Best Friends Forever

Kelly McKain

USBORNE

My
totally secret
journal
by
Lucy Jessica Hartley

Thursday the 3rd of November

at 6.24 p.m., in my room.

Hey girls!

I couldn't wait to write in here after Jules and Tilda left 'cos I have got something **A-MAZING** to tell you! Me and Jules and Tilda are totally *Skipping Through The Tulips* with excitedness about it (which is this phrase I have made up to mean we are *Over The Moon*, **BTW**). (And as you most probably know, **BTW** means *By The Way*, **BTW**!)

The totally exciting idea got thought up when me and Jules and Tilda were given the job of organizing this year's school disco. We didn't exactly *want* to do it, but Mr. Phillips said, "Any volunteers?" in assembly yesterday and there was this long massive silence and Tilda looked at me, then Jules, then grabbed our hands and stuck them

5

up, 'cos she felt bad for him that there were no volunteers. The reason there were no volunteers is 'cos the school disco is normally Not That Thrilling, and mainly involves some flat Coke and Sprite and a big bowl of crisps with the different kinds mixed up together so you don't know what you're getting (and if you accidentally end up with Wooster Sauce flavour you are grossed out for the rest of the evening – *shudder*). Plus the DJ is always just Mr. Bridges, our maths teacher, in a backwards baseball cap with a portable CD player. *Plus* the boys either do that stupid break-dancing by writhing around on the floor in a way that looks like they are trying to escape from a straitjacket, or they dance actually *with* you, which means going round and round in circles with their hands clamped on your bum. Not *très romantique*, as they most probably say in Paris.

So anyway, I am forgetting to tell you about our amazing idea. Whoops! Sorry! If you know me, you will already know that I am not exactly

fabulissimo at getting to the point! So, me,
T and J were sitting round my kitchen table trying
to think of ways to make the rubbish disco even
slightly groovy. I had made some coffee so we
would feel extra professional and businessy, like we
were having an officy meeting, but even that hadn't
worked. So, instead of having ideas, I was picking
off my nail polish, Jules was drawing a Celtic-style
tattoo on her arm in black biro, and Tilda was
flicking through the latest copy of our fave mag,
Hey Girls!

She was looking at this article about these high
school proms they have in America, and I was like,
"Come on, Tilda, stop reading about that cool
high school prom, we need to get back to work
and find a way to make our rubbish disco even
slightly groovy."

Then Tilda was staring at me and I didn't
know why.

Then I was staring at her and thinking,
I think I know what you're thinking.

7

Then Jules stopped tattooing herself and looked at the article and then at us with this face like, *I think I know what you two are thinking.*

And then at the same time we all exclaimed:

We could have a High School Prom!

I am sticking the *Hey Girls!* article in this journal so you can see what I am remotely on about.

Hey Girls!

Check out our stateside sisters from Echo Falls High School, California!

Destiny, Riley and Autumn (below) are all glammed up for their high school prom! With the help of a top interior designer the gym has been transformed into a prom night paradise, with silver curtains, hundreds of balloons and large arrangements of lilies and roses. Like Hollywood film stars, the girls enter on a red carpet, accompanied by their dates – yes, even the boys have

smartened up for the occasion! (See Bailey with Chad, above.) After sipping tropical fruit punch and enjoying delicate canapés, the girls have fun doing some elegant ballroom-style dancing with their partners. Then, after the prom king and queen are chosen, the lights go down, a famous DJ steps up to the decks and they dance the night away to top tunes!

Those American girls really know how to party in style!

So we are planning to have one of those!

Wow or what?!

We're going to let everyone have a vote on who should be prom queen and king, so it's democracy and fair.

Oh, Mum is calling me. I'm going to look after Alex (my little bro) while she goes to her meditation group. She's paying me two of the nail varnishes that she got as free samples (she's training to be a make-up artist and her college gets sent loads of  stuff to try out from the top brands — how cool!). I did ask her last week why she needs to do meditating when her life is so totally unstressful, and she absolutely burst out laughing for some weird reason.

Now that I am very actually 13 Mum trusts me to be in charge when she goes out — well, apart from texting every hour. So I have to go downstairs now and listen to her giving me the same instructions she does every time, like about how to tell if there's a gas leak and to look through the spyhole if the doorbell goes and **DO NOT OPEN THE DOOR** if it's someone I don't know (even if they have an official clipboard for doing a survey) and to **BE VERY CAREFUL** if I use the kettle and not to let Alex have more than two Wagon Wheels **AT THE VERY MOST**. I'm writing in capitals 'cos it always sounds like Mum is speaking in them. Isn't it weird how mums just totally worry about *everything* when you are in fact Quite Capable? *sigh!*

Anyway, will write more about our prom plans soon!

Bye!

11

8.24 p.m.

Hi again!

I'm just sitting on the sofa being in charge of
Alex, who is watching his *Power Rangers* DVD
and eating his third Wagon Wheel (whoopsie!).
I've made a list of the stuff we'll need for the
prom, and how much I think it will most likely
cost, and I'm sticking it in here so it doesn't
get lost. It took ages 'cos my mind kept wandering
off into ideas of what my prom dress would be like
– that is *soooooo* the most massively exciting bit!

(I estimated the costs with help from this box
on the second page of the *Hey Girls!* article that
told you what American-style proms cost.)

LIST OF STUFF WE NEED FOR THE PROM, AND
HOW MUCH I THINK IT WILL MOST LIKELY COST

<u>Posh catering firm</u> to do the canapés, which will
be like the ones we had at the wrap party for the
film we were in called <u>Passionate Indiscretions</u>:
asparagus wrapped in this stuff like wafer-thin ham
but redder, and this weeny naan bread with this
even weenier curry balanced on top, and also these
prawn vol-au-vents (which I have finally worked
out how to spell – yay!) and some smoked-salmon-
balanced-on-a-pancake thingamies. £1,000.
<u>Interior designer</u> to make the room look totally
WOW. £600.
<u>Famous DJ</u> from a cool London club. £1,500.
<u>Prom queen and king crowns</u> (probably silver,
with pearls and gems woven into the tiara?)
£500 each.
<u>Professional dance teachers</u> to show us some
ballroom moves, so we look cool like the celebs on
<u>Strictly Come Dancing</u>. About £500.
<u>Photographer,</u> one of those kind who normally
take photos of famous people for <u>Celeb</u> magazine.
£1,000.

So that means we can do it for about – hang on – yikes, £6,000! That is in fact quite a lot of *moolywonga*. Still, it will be *soooooo* cool and amazing and *soooooo* way better than the usual disco that maybe Mr. Phillips will agree.

Me, Tilda and Jules are meeting up in the loos before school tomorrow so they can throw any prom ideas of their own into the hat (not that there is an *actual* hat, but you get what I mean) and then we are going to knock on Mr. Phillips's office and ask him if we can have a prom.

GULP!

Fingers crossed he'll say yes!!!

PS We will also have to sing "Happy Birthday" to Jules in the morning, 'cos tomorrow she is turning 14 – **14!** Her family is having a big bonfire party on Saturday to celebrate, with fireworks and everything, and all the Hartleys and Van der Zwans are invited. How cool is that?!

PPS Gotta go and wrap Jules's pressie now!

14

Friday the 4th

Jules's birthday!

Just to quickly say that Jules loved her black nail varnish and henna tattoos that I got her and also the skull ring that Tilda bought her that looks like it could even be real silver. We all sang "Happy Birthday" really loudly and even the girls who were in the loo cubicles having a you-know-what joined in too, and even Jules did 'cos she never likes to be left out! So, after we had collapsed into giggles and then managed to get in control of ourselves, we had a quick prom chat and now we are sitting outside Mr. Phillips's office waiting to get called in.

Oh, erk, the door's opening – wish us luck!

Newsflash! Mr. Phillips
said yes to the prom!

I don't remember this but *apparently* when we
were telling him about our idea, I started going on
about how the normal disco is quite boring
because of all the going round and round in circles
with a boy's hands clamped onto your bum (I
can't believe I would have really said that to the
headmaster but Jules reckons I did and that
that's why she kicked me).

While I was going

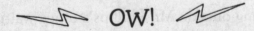 OW!

(and trying not to kick her back, but only 'cos it's
her birthday) Tilda took over with her info about
all the stuff we need. She had changed my list a bit
beforehand to make it only cost £2,000, but Mr.

Stingypants Phillips still said that
was too much and he is
only giving us £300, which
will not even buy half an
interior designer or half a
designed interior.

But at least he said yes!
Yippeeeeeee!!

We are going to look
soooooo amazing wearing
gorgeous prom dresses!!

I don't think we will be
having the asparagus thingies

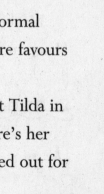

Half an interior
designer!

or the weeny curry on slighty-less-weeny bits
of naan bread, though. Still, Tilda says we can
definitely do something better than the normal
disco, we will just have to try and get more favours
from people, like help and stuff for free.

'Cos she is so brainy at it, we have put Tilda in
charge of all the maths from now on. Here's her
new list of what we need, which she copied out for

me and Jules. We are supposed to think of people who can help out and where we can get some of the things we need but for zero money.

Revised Prom List

Food and drinks - £200
Music and lights - £100
(That is all our money used up!)
Dancing teachers — free
Maybe prom queen and King crowns - free
Photographer - free
Flowers - free
Decorations - free
Red carpet - free

Maybe a Wagon Wheel will help me think…
Hang on…

2 mins later

Argh! I can't believe Alex has eaten them all!

Saturday the 5th

Yes! No school to get in the way of prom planning AND it's Jules's birthday bonfire party tonight!

Now I am going to write in here about the most important bit of the whole prom (for me, anyway!) —

MY DRESS!

I have decided to design and make my own glam prom dress — how totally cool is that?! I'm getting help from Nan (who likes to be called Delia, BTW, 'cos being called Nan makes her feel really old). Her actual job is making costumes for ballroom dancers so she is really fab at sewing and knows how to do v. v. complicated things, plus she always

19

has loads of sparkly sequins and beading stuff, so my dress will be mega-ly gorgeous!

I have to go in a mo (*oooooh*, that rhymes!) 'cos Jules and Tilda are coming over at 2 o'clock and it's 1.57 now. Jules wants me to help her with customizing this dress she already has and Tilda wants me to come up with ideas of what would suit her — her dad is buying her a brand-new dress and we are going shopping for it all together this week. Fab or what?! Even though Tilda's dad is v. v. stricty and a wearer of Embarrassing Sandals, I have to admit that he is quite nice sometimes, like when he let us do up Tilda's room into a swanky girl zone and then afterwards also let us have a fab sleepover.

For my dress, I have been looking for inspiration in Mum's old *Celeb* magazines that pile up by her bed. They always show A-list celebs and top models in these mega-ly gorge red-carpet dresses and I have cut out my faves this morning and laid them out on the kitchen table so I can get inspiration. Oh! I have just noticed that Mum has been writing notes on some of them! I'll stick them in here so you can see.

Don't even think about it, Lucy!

You're not going out like that until you're 18! And maybe not even then!

sigh!

Oh, gotta go, that is the doorbell ringing!

It is now 4.54 o'clock

(I can't believe it is
nearly dark already!)
and Jules and Tilda
have just gone home to
get ready for the bonfire party.

I did a total *faux pas* with Jules (which is French for massively putting your foot in it, BTW). In case you don't know, Jules is very Spanishly fiery and passionate, and 'cos of wanting to be an actress she is also very dramatic, so it's a bad idea to accidentally do a *faux pas* on her.

Anyway, she came round at 2.12 p.m. (Jules is always late but Tilda is always right on time so she had already been at my house for 12 mins). After we went upstairs, Jules took this dress out of a bag and (I am honestly not joking) it looked like this

23

Being as it was Halloween last Monday I just unthinkingly said, "Oh that would have been so cool for my Halloween costume instead of that stupid sheet I ended up wearing." (I'll explain more about that later.) "Why didn't you tell me you had this? Anyway, we're supposed to be thinking about cool prom dresses now, not Halloween stuff. Where's the one you want me to customize?"

Jules just stood there giving me this totally evil stare and I didn't realize why for ages (I'm so intensely immensely *dense* sometimes) and then Tilda said, "Lu, that *is* Jules's prom dress."

So then I was thinking *Yeeeek!* and I started saying how nice the dress was and how I was only joking about it looking like a Halloween costume. I also gabbled on about how much of a good idea it is for Jules to have something in her own style, which is Goth Rock Chick. Oh dear! I wish I wasn't **ALWAYS** putting my foot in it, but I usually am! Anyway, she smiled a tiny bit (phew!) and then she really cheered up when I started sketching some ideas of how we could make it work, like:

We also flicked through the *Celeb*
mags and my cut-out pix in this journal
and we had some ideas about colours
and styles that would look good on
Tilda. I think something like this →
in an emerald green or
champagne colour would look
amazing, and Tilda thought so too.

Then we had a properly serious
meeting about the prom organizational
stuff, with coffee and everything. Here
are our further organizational ideas:

Decorations – Mrs. Searle our art teacher
is really nice and she seems to actually LIKE
teenagers, which is weird for a teacher, so
maybe she'll help us with these.
Red carpet – still no ideas.
Food and drinks – still not sure how to
get fab food and drinks for only £2 per
person. 'Cos it is 100 people it is way too

many to make the food ourselves. But we did think about making our own cool cocktail-type drinks with all different fruit juices, like we had for this glam photo shoot we did once.

Music and lights – Mr. Phillips said we have to get a teacher to help us with this 'cos it involves electricals and also finding a DJ, so we are probably going to ask Mr. Wright, our English teacher.

Prom king and queen – I'm going to make crowns or something for them. We are going to have the voting on the prom night itself so it's a big surprise who's won. I hope it's not Jamie Cousins though, 'cos that would give him a bigger head than he has already!

Flowers – no ideas. Plus I have a horrible feeling that flowers are very expensive!

Photographer – ???

Ballroom dancing teachers – ???

27

So you can see we have got *some* ideas of how to do things but we still need loads more.

Before we got talking about the next subject, which was For Girls' Ears Only, I had to go and make sure Alex (my little bro) was not somehow spying on us. Luckily he was in his room practising his made-up karate (which is how he broke his lamp last week, which made Mum annoyed because it was quite expensive and also Electrically Dangerous, as well as being just Normally Dangerous from the glass bits).

But anyway.

If you too have a little bro you will probably get why I didn't want him to hear us talking about the highly secret subject of (shhh!) *dates with actual boys* (i.e. 'cos he would start teasing me and go on and on and *ooooooon* about it for *ever*, or at least until I had paid him about 7 packets of Fruit Pastilles to shut up).

It's not like any of us three **BFF** have got an actual person we want to go with (yet!) but the whole conversation got so funny 'cos we were all suggesting boys for each other, like going:

Yurgh, not him!

You know Daniel Archer told me he fancies you, Lu. Maybe you should go with him?

I wish Bill Cripps wasn't already going out with Augusta Rinaldi, 'cos that means they'll definitely be going together, and he is quite okayish.

We were all agreeing with that 'cos Bill Cripps is the most okay of all the okay boys in our class — well, along with Jamie Cousins and Ben Jones.

Speaking of Ben Jones, me and him sometimes muck about in the cloakroom when we have to put our coats away after breaktime – like, he always grabs my jacket and pulls it over my head and tries to make me fall on the floor, so I smack him one because then I have to go back into the loos and do my hair again and get in trouble for being late for lessons and that. So maybe *he* fancies me. (Or actually maybe he hates me, and the jacket thing is because he is trying to suffocate me into dropping dead?!)

When any of us suggested someone we were getting more and more into giggles until we were in total hysterics (which Mum calls *getting the sillies*) and we could hardly stop laughing for long enough to even say any more boys' names.

Then Tilda said, "What about Simon Driscott, Lucy?" and me and Jules collapsed into more giggles 'cos Simon Driscott is this boy who I used to call the Prince of Pillockdom but who I have gradually found out is quite funny and okay.

30

When I stopped nearly dying from laughter,
I managed to say, "Duh! Simon Driscott is just my
sort of friend with no fancying going on whatsoever,
so how could I ask him out as my date?!"

Jules went, "Yeah, you can't go on a date with
a mate! It has to be a *boy*-type boy."

Tilda said she hadn't realized that and that's
why she'd said the thing about Simon Driscott,
which is weird 'cos she is v. v. clever and normally
realizes stuff way before me and Jules do, like
answers to maths homework questions and the
capitals of different countries and the chemical
symbols of the periodic table (me and Jules are
usually too busy trying not to giggle in science
whenever Mrs. Stepton says *periodic table* so we
aren't listening exactly *properly*. BTW, we have
got a code word, well, a code letter for actual
periods, which is Q, so we can talk about them
even when boys are there. I haven't got mine yet
but J and T have, which is really annoying, and I
have this secret worry that mine will probably not

turn up till I am massively old, like about 25 or something, and I'll end up in the *Guiness Book of Records* so everyone will know and it will be the biggest CRINGE of all CRINGES in the history of everything ever. *shudder!*).

So we all said we have got no particular boy in mind, and I do really mean it, but I am secretly wondering if Jules and Tilda are just saying that, 'cos when I went, "Tell me now honestly if you two have people you like," Tilda blushed a bit and Jules was weirdly silencio and she picked all the black nail polish off her right-hand little finger. So...I will have to keep my eyes and ears extra open in case I spot any clues that they do in fact fancy specific boys after all!

Yikes, I've just seen the time – gotta go and get ready for Jules's party. *Byeeee!*

32

<u>Saturday at 12.24 p.m.,</u>
oh, sorry, I mean a.m.,
like, in the middle of the
night when it changes
to Sunday. Oh, so
it is Sunday!

There is loads to tell you about Jules's bonfire party! Thinking about it all is making me not be able to sleep so I may as well write everything down in here now.

When we first got to Jules's us three had a good time inventing fruit punches for the prom by mixing different juices together, and we came up with three delish ones. They are:

<u>Apple Cooler:</u>
Apple juice, crushed ice,
squeeze of lime juice,
sprig of mint

33

<u>Purple Sunrise</u>:
Orange juice, ice cubes, layer of blackcurrant (Mum showed me how to pour it down the back of a spoon to make it stay at the bottom. She said it was a little trick she picked up in Mexico a long, long time ago, and then she couldn't stop grinning)

<u>Tropical Paradise</u>:
Pineapple, mango, lemonade, ice, frozen bits of pineapple and glacé cherries on a stick.
Cool idea to freeze the fruit, huh? Tilda's dad suggested that. He said it was a little tip he picked up in Barbados in the 80s and then <u>he</u> started chuckling too. I <u>so</u> do not get adults sometimes!

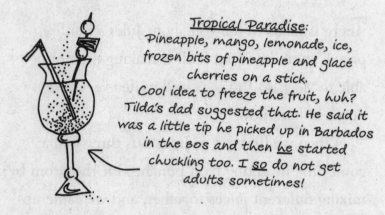

Then we went outside to have the bonfire and the fireworks in Jules's jungly garden. Apparently, Jules's dad has what Mum calls "The Spanish Attitude To Health And Safety" and while he was setting up the fireworks, she spent the whole time cringing behind her jacket potato and expecting his hand to come flying off at any second.

34

Actually, I have just realized that I am feeling quite artistic at the mo so I think I'll draw you some pix as well. This is us three **BFF** linking arms and watching the fireworks:

At first we were acting like we were too old to go *oooooooohh* and *aaaaaaaaahh* and that, but then we forgot about our very actually 13ness (and Jules's 14ness!) and it was really exciting and we were doing just about the biggest ooohs and ahhhs of everyone.

This is the yummy food we had:

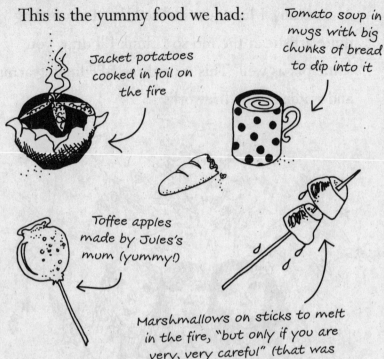

Jacket potatoes cooked in foil on the fire

Tomato soup in mugs with big chunks of bread to dip into it

Toffee apples made by Jules's mum (yummy!)

Marshmallows on sticks to melt in the fire, "but only if you are very, very careful" (that was Mum saying that bit, obviously!)

After the food and the fireworks, Mum relaxed a bit more 'cos no one had yet lost a limb, and she didn't even seem to mind that much when Dad got out his guitar. (He was invited to the party because he was also friends with Jules's family before him and Mum got separated. I can't believe it's been over a year since they split up. I used to get really upset about it but I am kind of okayish about it now – most of the time, anyway.)

Normally Mum is not a big fan of Dad's singing (when he started doing the, like, about 10 verses of "American Pie" at our Rock Party this one time, she threatened to embed a sausage roll in his head). I was kind of wishing there were sausage rolls to use as missiles tonight 'cos when Dad started singing I was just thinking, CRINGE!!!

Okay, I admit that he has improved a lot technically-wise and he doesn't hurt your ears as much now, but he was doing one of those songs that is all seriously about lurve and he was doing it in this way like he really meant all the words, and going "Ooooooh baby, you drive me crazy"

with his eyes closed while shaking his head about and that sort of thing.

shudder!

Not only was it as cheesy as one of Jules's fave sandwiches, but I don't like the idea of my dad having emotional feelings like a normal person when he is supposed to be just a dad. When he finished, everyone clapped, maybe 'cos he was good and maybe 'cos he had stopped, I'm not really sure. Then he said, "Any requests?" and Jules's granny said, "How about 'Living Doll'?" (which is this song that the Older Generation like) and Mum said, "How about '*Russian* Doll'?"

I did a snort of laughter 'cos that was her secretly mentioning when my dad recently had a date with this Russian lady called Veruschka. I was scared she would become my wicked stepmother but it didn't work out – phew!

When Mum said the *Russian Doll* comment, Dad went red and handed the guitar on to Jules's dad Gabriel instead, who started doing this Spanishly flamenco music on it. Dad was in a big mood with Mum, but then she did that nudging his shoulder thing you do when you're trying to get someone out of a bad mood, while going, "Oh, Brian, I'm only teasing!" Luckily instead of staying in the mood, Dad grinned and told her to watch it in future or he'd do "American Pie" with all the verses and *then* she'd be sorry. I'm so glad they are getting on well(-ish!) now, even if it is only as friends.

We all tried to dance to Jules's dad playing the Spanish music, and it was really fun, apart from us nearly falling over 'cos of our heels sticking in the mud.

Then Gabriel passed the guitar to JJ (Jules's brother, who I have had a massivo *hsurc terces* on in the past, but luckily I am over that now, although I have to tell you he is amazing at playing the guitar and he did look really heart-throbby sitting there strumming away in the firelight!).

Jules's dad made her mum put the tray of stuffed peppers down and soon they were doing this amazing Latin dance with loads of swishing and swirling of her skirt and stamping of his feet and arms in the air over their heads. I was just staring at them with my eyes popping out of my head, thinking, *Wow, I know they go to classes every week but I didn't realize they had become so good!* and Jules was also staring at them with her eyes popping out of her head and quietly groaning, "Oh, why are parents *sooooooo* embarrassing?"

After that, Jules's mum disappeared into the kitchen and came out carrying this massive chocolate fudge cake in the  shape of a bat, with 14 candles stuck in the wings. JJ started playing "Happy Birthday" and we all joined in with singing for Jules. When she blew out the candles she made a wish, but she won't even tell us BFF what it was in case the magic gets ruined.

When we were all getting a bit cold we went indoors and Jules put on this DVD of us on the *Go Green!* TV show, talking about the eco-friendly makeover we did on Tilda's room a couple of weeks ago (it's not on *actual* TV for 3 more months but the nice production people sent us an advance copy to show everyone). It was really cool and also weird, 'cos I was seeing myself in a new way, like, from the outside, how other people must see me. I looked older than I imagined, and my new smile I'd been practising looked really nice. Everyone clapped at the end and we all did a bow.

Okay, I am feeling less buzzy and much more tired now I've written all that, so I'm going to sleep.

Goodnight!

Sunday (again) but now morning at 10:34 a.m.

Sundays are supposed to be family day, so I am not allowed to go and hang out with Jules and Tilda, but it's not too bad 'cos they are busy anyway. Like, Jules still has some aunties and cousins staying round after last night and they are having a big paella and probably arguing in really fast Spanish like normal.

Poor Tilda, her mum died when she was little, so it's just her and her dad. They do activities together on Sundays 'cos he works really hard the rest of the time. Usually it is things of Cultural Importance, such as visiting the Iron Age hill fort near Dorchester and going on beach walks in the freezing wind in Lyme Regis to look for fossils. After us three **BFF** went on holiday together and Mr. Van der Zwan made us walk up this massive hill in this lashing rain wearing these **CAGOULES**

42

(no, really, I am not joking!) I would never want
to go on one of his trips out again. I know you are
thinking, *Eeekkk! Poor Tilda!* but don't worry
'cos as she is really brainy, she actually *enjoys*
stuff like that.

Normally, me and Alex see Dad on Sundays.
Sometimes we see Nan as well, 'cos Dad goes
round there to do his washing (he has somehow
remembered to buy a red convertible sports car,
but keeps forgetting to order a washing machine).
He used to live with Uncle Ken in this manky
flat up loads of stairs that smelled of curry and
feet but now he has moved into his own place
(or "pad" as he embarrassingly calls it!) 'cos he
can afford it since he became a DJ at our local
radio station.

Anyway, I am going off the point again – soz!
I like going to Nan's 'cos we can talk about clothes
and stylishness and that, plus when I am doing a
project like making a Fantasy Fashion outfit (which
I did for this one competition), she helps me with

the hard bits. When we go round there on Dad days she makes us all proper Sunday lunch, which is cool. (So is what we do when it's just Dad, which is go to Pizza Hut, but Nan's is still better.)

Today Dad is at a classic car rally with Uncle Ken and Alex. I was going too, but when they came to get us, I suddenly got a mysterious headache that struck like lightning as if from nowhere, and it was v. v. agony-making. Luckily it has gone away now, and in the end it worked out quite well 'cos I would way rather stay here and work on my dress designs than go round looking at old cars anyway, especially 'cos Dad insists on patting the bonnets and calling them "she" as if they are actual living people. CRINGE!!!

About 7.30-ish

I can't see the clock
from here.

We got back from Nan's a while ago. Dad rang
up about 4 o'clock to say they were back from the
car rally and as I felt so much better Mum took
me round to Nan's and she stayed while we had
a salady tea.

I showed Nan the designs I'd done, and she
liked them all but she said that some would look
better than others when they were made up, so
that eliminated a couple. We chose the best one
and made some changes to the cut and talked
about materials and that, and then while Alex
was showing Dad his made-up karate in the
conservatory and Mum and Nan were chatting
in the kitchen I went and sat in the living room
to think quietly and I drew out the final design,
which is like this ⟶

45

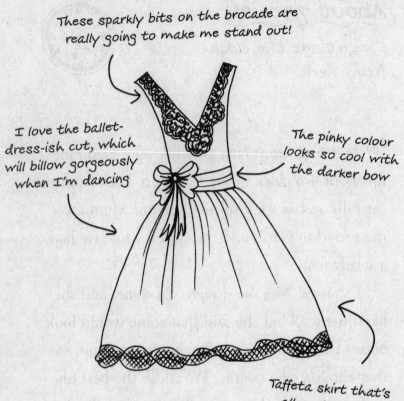

These sparkly bits on the brocade are really going to make me stand out!

I love the ballet-dress-ish cut, which will billow gorgeously when I'm dancing

The pinky colour looks so cool with the darker bow

Taffeta skirt that's all rustly when I walk

Fab or what?! My stomach flips with excitement every time I imagine me walking into the prom in that dress!!! It's the sort of dress that Keira Knightley would wear to a premiere. I reckon it will make the girls all go, "Wow! You

46

look amazing!" and plus, the boys will just be silently staring at me with their eyeballs popping out of their heads.

I'm going to imagine that happening a bit more, but I need to close my eyes for the best effect so I'll have to stop writing in here now – so *byeeeeee*!!!

Monday the 7th

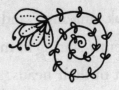

$\mathcal{U}$s three **BFF** are the total Ace Team of Prom Planning, especially Tilda. She is like a speeding bullet of organization 'cos last night she had the idea of asking the dinner ladies to do the buffet for the prom and so she fixed up a meeting at first break with Gladys and Beryl.

I've stuck in our original list of food things that we wanted. Tilda worked it out when she got back from her Excursion of Historical Interest yesterday, and me and Jules added our own ideas to it in morning registration and then I copied it out so I could keep it safely in here with all the other prom stuff.

* Sausages on sticks
* Cheese and pineapple on
  sticks (which sounds weird but
  you have to have it at
  any kind of party)
* Pizza slices or
  maybe mini pizzas
* The salmon-balanced-on-pancake
  thingies (it would be good to have at
  least one posh canapé!)
* Frazzle et Wotsit skewers,
  which are my own invention
  that I made up
* Dairylea avec cucumber à la
  Ritz cracker (I made that
  up too, it's yummy!)

49

* Chocolate fingers

* Bacon crisps (they are Tilda's
  fave and she's not allowed
  them at home 'cos of her
  dad being mega-ly stricty
  about Healthy Eating)

* Mini cheese sandwiches, but with the
  crusts cut off and a cocktail stick sticking
  through them to be more party-ish. (Jules
  added this idea 'cos cheese sandwiches
  are her faviest thing ever and she said if
  Tilda is having bacon crisps then she is
  having cheese sandwiches.)

* Wagon Wheels ('cos if they are
  both having a faviest thing on
  the list then I am too!)

'Cos of our budget being really tiny, Gladys and Beryl just wanted to do a big bowl of all different flavour crisps mixed up again, which is horrible for the Wooster Sauce reasons I have mentioned before. But luckily Tilda is a tough ~~negoshiashionist~~ – no, hang on, that can't be right – ~~negoshiationist~~ ~~negotiationist~~ good at getting what she wants.

There has just been about a 4 minute and 24 second break since I wrote that last bit, BTW

ARGH! Typical! I was just minding my own business quietly writing in here when Simon Driscott leaned over my shoulder and saw what I was writing and went, "Actually it's N.E.G.O.T.I.A.T.O.R."

GRRRRRR!!! It's so annoying when he corrects me — he thinks he is the _Fountain of all Knowledge_, like →

I snapped my journal shut and went, "Yes, can I help you?"

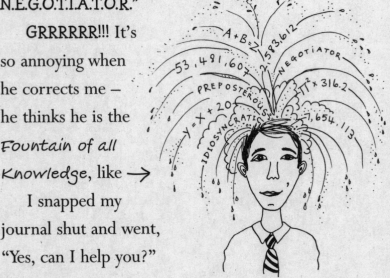

Instead of looking all smug like he normally does 'cos of knowing everything in the entire universe, Simon Driscott looked all red and flustery and he kept opening and closing his mouth like a fish but no words were coming out. Then just when I was about to go back to writing in here he went, "About the prom...erm, I'm just wondering, er, well, erm, have you got anyone to go with yet?"

I explained that I haven't even hardly *thought* about date-type stuff 'cos of having to do all the organizing for the music and food and decorations, and he said, "Maybe I can make it easier for you."

That's when I got struck with the *Creative Inspiration* that Simon Driscott would be the perfect person to help Mr. Wright sort out the music and lights side of things, 'cos of technologicality being his favest thing ever. I went, "Great! Thanks for offering! I need you to help Mr. Wright find a good DJ for only about 100 quid which is our entire music budget. And also, if you could design the lighting and get the Geeky Minions, whoops, I mean your Charming Friends, to put the rigs up like they did for my charity fashion show that would be excellent."

Simon seemed a bit weird after that, like he didn't really *want* to do the DJ-finding or design the lighting, which is odd seeing as he'd just offered to help me. Huh! And people say *girls* are moody and unpredictable!

Anyway, as I was saying before I was so **RUDELY INTERRUPTED** by SD, Gladys and Beryl reckon they can't possibly do even our revised menu with our food budget of £200. I know it sounds a lot, but there are about 100 people in our year so that is only about £2 per person and that includes the drinks as well.

Plus, they wanted us to have loads of salad and vegetable quiches and that, 'cos of Healthy Eating, but we thought that sounded *soooooo* boring, i.e. more like a dieting party than a High School Prom. For a compromise, we have agreed to have crudités, which are basically chopped-up vegetables that you dunk in a yogurty sauce, and plus they are putting peppers and mushrooms on top of the mini pizzas as well as just cheese. They aren't doing the Frazzle et Wotsit skewers, 'cos it is too hard to make hundreds of them stick on the skewers without crumbling, but they did say yes to just bowls of bacon crisps so Tilda is happy at least. (And BTW, it was yes to cheese sandwiches, so Jules is too, but no to my choice of Wagon Wheels – boo!)

'Cos we can't afford the smoked salmon things, we have agreed on mini chicken drumsticks instead. For pudding (which we hadn't even thought of – whoops!) there are going to be cupcakes and fruit skewers, which look like this ———→

Healthy but scrummy!

We told Gladys and Beryl about our ideas for different fruit punches and they said they will buy in whatever juices we need to make them up, and at the prom they will be served in big bowls and maybe even have bits of fruit floating about in them – how cool!

BTW, Chantelle just went past and said, "Oh hi, Lucy, Stefano Stefanopolis fancies you." Huh! How interesting! He's not in my class so I don't know him very well but he seems quite nice. Maybe he'll ask me to the prom!

Monday at 7.54 p.m.

I am lying on my bed
scoffing sweets left over
from Halloween last week.
Yum!

I'm actually glad I ended up going Trick or
Treating with Alex now – these sweets are really
nice! Alex was meant to be going with his friend
Matthew, whose mum was supposed to come round
and take them both out, but Matthew got some
kind of disgusting lurgy so she couldn't. I didn't
really want to go because of Trick or Treating being
for children and not Very Actual Teenagers and I
was worried that someone from school might see
me and think I was doing it for my own benefit.
But Alex was looking so sad all dressed up and
ready to go in his Harry Potter costume (since
Mum bought it for him it is his fave thing to wear
even just normally after school) and plus, Mum was
getting stressed out 'cos she was really busy with

this bit of homework that she had to give in for her make-up artist course.

When I said I would go, Mum was like, "Thanks, Lu, I'll treat you to a new lipgloss for doing this."

I said, "I'm not doing it to get a reward — this is just the sort of Model Daughter I am." But then I quickly added, "But don't take that to mean I don't actually want the new Sheer Shine Glide-On Strawberry Shake Juicy Lips, seeing as you're offering."

So I made myself a ghost costume by getting an old white sheet (well, it was mostly white apart from the bit of pattern, but that had been washed so often you could hardly see it) and cutting out eye holes, like this ——>

58

Then I put some sparkly eye make-up on and started experimenting with swooshy liquid eyeliner, seeing as my eyes were the only bit of me anyone would see. Alex was going, "Come on, Lu, hurry up, or all the sweets will be gone and there'll only be fruit left," so I was just about to go, but then I caught sight of myself in the mirror and gave myself a fright – not 'cos the ghost costume was scary (obviously!) but because it was *soooooo* frumpy and I looked *awful*! So I tried adding a belt and some accessories like this

The problem was that then I didn't look like a ghost any more, but just like a girl who for some strange reason had decided to wear a slightly-patterny sheet with eye holes cut out of it. But by then Alex was getting all panicky about only getting

59

fruit and in the end Mum just had to shove us out of the door. Luckily everyone in our street (which is the only place we were allowed to go knocking) still had actual sweets left and we got a big stash (I thought I might as well take a bag with me too, seeing as I had to go anyway). When we got in, Alex said I was the best sister in the world, which was a miracle, so I wrote it down and made him sign it. I've had it Blu-tacked to my door all week, but I'd better stick it in here for safety in case Alex rips it down.

Lucy Jessica Hartley is the Best
Sister In The (Entire) World.
Signed:

A Lexander James
Hartley

True!

Next time he says I am a big poo pants for making us watch *Friends* on E4 instead of his *Monster Trucks* DVD I will get this journal out and show him that I am in fact the *Best Sister In The (Entire) World.* **HA-HA-HAAAAAA!!!**

Evil-genius laugh!!!

Whoops, I have just noticed that I've been going on loads and looooads about Halloween. I'm right now going to get on with what I'm meant to be doing, which is looking in my book called *Crafty Things To Make And Do* for ideas for party decorations, 'cos this afternoon Miss Searle said yes to helping us with them.

Tuesday

*U*s three BFF got *sooooo* giggly and silly today after lunch that my sides almost actually *split* from laughing so much, even though I used to think that was only a saying. So I have come into the loos for the last bit of outside time to write in this journal, 'cos we have got a meeting with Mr. Phillips at afternoon registration about the prom and I *soooooo* can't end up hysterically giggling in his office!

What happened was, we'd been on first lunch and afterwards we were sitting in the little doorway round the back of the art room, which is our second fave place to hang out (here in the loos is our *no. 1* place, of course!). We were talking about which boys to go to the prom with again, and we all still said we hadn't thought of anyone. That was when Jules came up with this idea to do a dating agency type thing. She made me get some paper out of the back of my maths book and then us two voted that Tilda should be the first one we tried it out on. She was going, "That is so unfair, two against one!" but I was going, "It *is* fair because one vote each is democracy which is the most fairest of fair things that you can get."

So we made up some questions to find Tilda's perfect prom date, and I am sticking them in here for you to see:

They got one point for each right answer, BTW

Dating Agency Questionnaire

Do you like:

1) Naturey stuff

2) Reading massivo books of historical interest

3) Cool girls with nice wavy blonde hair

4) Wearing your trousers hanging halfway down your bum so your pants are constantly showing ←

This is a trick question 'cos Tilda hates that!

5) Doing loud botty burps in public and then saying, "Better out than in!" ←

Tilda hates that too!

6) Really hard maths questions

7) Opening doors for girls while going, "Ladies first"

8) And are you funny? (As in funny ha-ha not funny weird)

63

When we'd finally stopped giggling enough to even speak, we got into our positions. I sat in the little doorway round the back of the art room and Tilda hid round the side by the recycling bins and Jules went marching off to find boys to answer our questionnaire. Jamie Cousins and Ben Jones both came without her having to pull them along, and also  Danny Jacobs, although he massively failed the test by only getting 1 point out of 8 so he is definitely not the right date for Tilda (and the 1 right was question 8 and even though the teachers are always going, "Danny Jacobs, are you trying to be funny?" when he's making parp noises under his arm in class, that's not the kind of funny Tilda likes).

Ben Jones and Jamie Cousins each got 4 out of 8, which is not too bad. Ben Jones asked if it meant *I'd* go out with him! I'm not sure if he meant it as a serious question or a joke (sometimes

64

it is impossible to tell with boys, isn't it?) so I just laughed. Maybe if he does want to go to the prom together, though, he'll ask me properly. When I read out the blonde hair question, Jamie Cousins went, "Are you talking about Tilda Van der Zwan?" and I said, "Yes" by accident. It just came out even though the questionnaire was supposed to be secretly anonymous and Tilda went, "Lucy!!" from round behind the recycling bins. But then Jamie Cousins said loudly, "In that case definitely yes, 'cos she is well fit, man," and Tilda did a big scream and giggle which set me and Jules completely off into hysterics and I could hardly speak to ask him the rest of the questions. She wouldn't seriously want to go with JC though, cos he totally loves himself!

Then we ran out of boys who wanted to do a dating questionnaire from their own free will, so Jules and Tilda came back into the little doorway and Jules said to Ben Jones and Jamie Cousins, "Go and get Adam and Jake!" and so they did.

Adam and Jake didn't really take the questions very seriously and Tilda was covering her face with her hands and going all red but still helplessly giggling and it was *soooooo* funny my face was really hurting from laughing so much.

Then we sent Ben and Jamie to get Harry and Abdul and their lot from 9L and to save time when they said "yes" to a no question or "no" to a yes question we started going, "**BEEP**, that is the wrong answer, **NEXT**!!!" and sending them away.

Tilda was crying with laughter and also embarrassment 'cos the questionnaire was so obviously about her, and screeching, "Lucy, please stop!"

I didn't want to 'cos it was so much fun but eventually we ran out of boys. Ben Jones and Jamie Cousins went off to play football (well, I mean with a tennis ball 'cos they are not allowed actual footballs in the playground) and we finally managed to calm down before one of us burst an eye or something.

Jules said, "Oh, I wish we hadn't run out of boys," and then Tilda said really shyly, "Well, you haven't done *all* the boys," and then shoved her face in her sleeve straight away to hide her bright-red-ness, so we knew that something was UP. I had to use my BFF skills to convince her to tell us what it was by saying, "We're your BFF and if you tell us which boy to bring round here we're not going to be all stupid about it, we promise, and plus we should have no secrets from each other," etc.

So then Tilda said, "Well, maybe you could get Sanjit."

Me and Jules both massively wanted to jump around squealing, but 'cos we had promised to be sensible we had to restrain ourselves and just do raised eyebrows at each other. But inside we were thinking,

EEEEEEEEEEEEEEKKKKKKKKKKK!!!!!!

WE KNOW WHO TILDA FANCIES!!!!!!

So Sanjit came over and he got 6 out of the 8 questions right and at the end I went,

"Congratulations, you are our top scorer. Would you like to go to the prom with Tilda Van der Zwan?" and Tilda was going, "Lucy! Shut UP!" but when Sanjit went, "Yeah, okay," she didn't go, "No way, I'm not going with him!" or anything. Instead, she just went even bright redder than exploding volcano lava and when he had disappeared back round the corner we all had the biggest squealy hug you have ever seen, and even though Tilda kept going, "Lucy! I can NOT believe you just asked him straight out like that, I am SO embarrassed!" I could tell she was really pleased. So now one of us has got a date at least. Hey, I just realized — if I didn't already want to be a *Real Actual Fashion Designer* when I grow up, I could start a dating agency!

Right, that is the bell going. Jules and Tilda have just knocked on my loo cubicle and said time to go and see Mr. P — luckily I am feeling less hysterical now so I won't embarrass myself in front of him.

<u>The Poor Law of 1834</u>

I am supposed to be doing history but I just wanted to quickly write about how the meeting with Mr. Phillips went. I will do it in bullet points for speediness and sorry if I suddenly have to stop writing 'cos Mrs. Smith has spotted that I am not doing the stuff on the board.

1) We got there and we were sitting in Mr. Phillips's office and the secretary came in and said, "Would you like some coffee?" so I was like, "A skinny cappuccino please, but if you haven't got one of those special machines I don't mind just a normal coffee, white with two sugars and if poss one of those biscuits you get on trains that come in the individual

69

wrappers. OW!" The "OW!" was 'cos Jules had kicked me (why is she always doing that?!) and I realized Tilda was bugging her eyeballs out at me and then Mr. Phillips cleared his throat and said, "Actually, I think Debbie was talking to _me_, Lucy." CRINGE!!!

2) I have just noticed that the above bullet point was not very bullety or pointy. Sorry.

3) I had to start a new one or the one above would not have been very bullety or pointy either.

4) We reported to Mr. P about the food and drink and music and lights being in the process of getting sorted out, and how Mrs. Searle is helping us with the decorations and that.

5) We explained that the main thing we are stuck on is how to find professional ballroom

70

dancing teachers, 'cos when Tilda checked on the net they are about £50 per single session and we would need quite a few lessons and plus we have nearly spent all our budget already, HINT HINT.

6) I had meant to just think the HINT HINT bit but instead it ended up coming out of my mouth in actual words. But still, Mr. P ignored the hint to give us more money and instead he just said he remembers Mrs. Stepton (who is our science teacher) doing some sort of evening class involving ballroom dancing and he'll ask her if she can help out.

7) So now it is only the flowers and the photographer that we have absolutely zilchio idea about how to sort out.

8) Gotta go - Mrs. S coming over!

71

Tuesday night

I have to do my history that I didn't finish in class 'cos of writing about the prom stuff, but first I have got some amazing girl goss to tell you that just cannot wait one single minute longer. After school, me, Jules and Tilda all went shopping together to look for Tilda's perfect prom dress. It was raining a bit but in fact that made it even more fun because we were all trying to squish under Tilda's umbrella so our hair didn't go crazy.

We went to New Look first and tried some stuff on but there was nothing quite right – I did see some fab bracelets, though, like

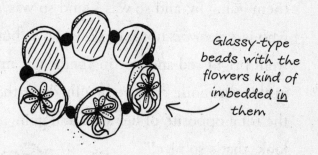

Glassy-type beads with the flowers kind of imbedded _in_ them

I have bought one to wear to the prom.

Then we went down to Girlsworld, which is this fab boutique-type shop run by this lovely lady called Cindy who is just totally cool. When we did our picture-perfect fashion shoot for the school mag she let me and Jules wear her stuff ('cos we were being the models) and then she even put big posters of us up in the shop!

So, we were just standing outside there staring at the fab dresses in the window display and these boys called Marcus and Cosmo from our class went past, who are in the lot that do skateboarding and have their jeans hanging really low down off their bums so you can see their pants all the time. I know you are thinking, *so what?* about them going by, and so was I, and so was Tilda, who is *sooooooo* not into sk8er boyz, but *Jules* went bright red and starting being v. v. interested in this turquoise coloured ruffly dress that was the total opposite of her style and going, "Oh, look, that's so nice!"

Then she grabbed me and Tilda's hands and dragged us into the shop and Tilda tried on the turquoise ruffly dress. It looked really good on her, like

But it wasn't The One.

While Tilda was trying on two other dresses I was still thinking *hmmm* about Jules's strange reaction to the boys going past, so I decided to do a test by going, "Jules, you know you loved that turquoise ruffly dress so much? Why don't you try it on, just for fun?"

Now, I have been **BFF** with Jules since we were five years old, when we got tied together for the three-legged race and won it because of our cooperational skills, so I know her well enough to be 100% sure that there is no way in a million years she liked that dress for herself or that she would try on a turquoise ruffly dress ever, ever, ever. She went, "No, I don't think I will, thanks," and kept coming up with rubbish excuses and I kept going, "Oh, go on, go on, go on," until she finally cracked under the pressure and went, "Okay! I don't like the dress! I was just trying to hide from Cosmo!"

I was grinning like ten Cheshire cats who got the cream then 'cos my cunning plan was working.

75

"And why were you trying to hide from him?"
I asked.

Just then, Tilda came out of the changing cubicle in the second dress, which was lovely.

Coral satin
and chiffon
puffball
stylie

"Why were you trying to hide from who?" she asked.

"Cosmo," I said.

"That dress is lovely, but not The One," said Jules.

"Don't try to change the subject," said Tilda. "Anyway, no way would I wear this, 'cos of it being so short."

Jules sighed and went, "Okay, fine. Cosmo is my secret crush and I really want to ask him to the prom but I don't know if he likes me so I don't want to ask him in case he says no and I just completely curl up with CRINGITIS, so I didn't know what to do, and when I see him it makes me completely curl up with CRINGITIS anyway."

"We could do a dating agency questionnaire about you on him," Tilda suggested, but Jules said no way José and how that would be *far* too embarrassing. Tilda was like, "Oh thanks, so it would be far too embarrassing for you but it was fine for me!" But she was only pretending to be annoyed 'cos she has got her date with Sanjit and she couldn't help doing a little smile even though she was trying really, really hard not to.

Then Tilda went back into the changing rooms to try on the third dress and when she came out we completely forgot that boys even *exist* 'cos we were too busy staring at her in **FLABBERGASTED GOBSMACKEDNESS** because she looked so amazingly beautiful and elegant, like this:

That dress is so definitely *The One* and Cindy has put it out the back for Tilda's dad to come and buy.

Later on when we were in Boots trying on make-up, Jules said a really surprising thing. I was just rubbing some Ruby Tuesday lipgloss on the back of my hand and I said, "Oh, this looks nice, shall I put some actually *on* you, Jules?" and she said, "Whatever, it's not like it will make any difference anyway. You two will always be way prettier than me whatever I do."

Me and Tilda were in complete GOBSMACKED FLABBERGASTATION when she said that 'cos we just could not believe she would think that – Jules is so nice and bubbly and plus she has brilliant hair and lovely big eyes with long lashes.

We said all that of course but she was still really gloomy and she said, "I wish I was pretty and girly like you. But I'm too loud and tomboyish and weird-looking and that's why I haven't got a date and you two have."

"I haven't either!" I went, but Jules said, "But Ben Jones will probably ask you out any minute.

79

He so obviously fancies you."

"And Stefano Stefanopolis from Mrs. Wade's class likes me too, according to Chantelle," I replied, and then Tilda gave me a *shut up* look and I felt really bad and wished my brain would *think* before it opened my mouth and let words come out.

"Well, *zero* boys fancy *me*," said Jules, close to tears. She kicked the make-up stand with the toe of her DM and added, "I'm fed up of being me. I wish I was someone different."

Tilda put her arm round Jules and said, "You're perfect exactly the way you are. You wouldn't be Jules if you changed a single thing. You just need to find the right boy for you, that's all. And maybe it's Cosmo, and maybe he's thinking he'd like to ask you out but he's worrying that *you* don't fancy *him*. So maybe you need to make the first move."

"Yes, exactly," I added. Tilda is so great at knowing what to say in a crisis, it's better if I just agree with her and don't try to add anything in case I end up putting my foot in it (which you have probably noticed I have a habit of doing – CRINGE!!).

A big fat tear spilled over and rolled down Jules's cheek, making a trail of the Black Magic mascara she'd been trying on run all down her face. But still, she smiled a tiny smile as she wiped it away with her sleeve. "Maybe," she said.

So after that me and Tilda carried on our mission of cheering her up by doing her make-up in Boots using the testers and telling her more examples of how fab she is until she said, "Enough already, I think I can actually feel my head swelling up! I'm not going to get out the door at this rate."

"Oh, you'll be okay," I said helpfully. "They're those massive sliding shop doors after all."

"Charming!" Jules cried and punched my arm and we all had a giggle when I realized what I'd said. (I did just warn you about me putting my foot in it, didn't I?!)

Then when we'd tested out the body sprays and picked our faves ('cos we have to *smell* nice for the prom too!), Tilda's dad came to get her and dropped me and Jules off home on his way back to theirs.

It's amazing that even with your very, very bestest friends there are sometimes things that you don't know. I have always thought that Jules was the most mega-confident one of us and it turns out that she doesn't feel that way at all! I hope she feels better now that we have had the big **BFF** chat though. And I hope she dares to ask Cosmo out.

Erk! It's 8.05 already and I haven't even started my history. I was planning to have it done by now and be thinking about table decorations for the prom, and how to do up the hall and that, but time is going **TICK TICK TICK!!!** I will have to **FOCUS** on the organizing from tomorrow morning or it won't matter if we have nice dresses and hair and make-up and smell nice and have cool dates because we'll get to the prom and there will be just the dusty old hall and some gym equipment and some Year 7s doing forward rolls to get their BAGA badges. **BTW**, I have never *got* that – I mean, just because you stand up and do that *tada!* thing, like

after doing a forward roll, that doesn't make it *gymnastics*. It is still only a forward roll.

Anyway, why am I going on about forward rolls when there is urgent history and prom organizing to do?! Actually I think I'll go straight on to planning the decorations and just copy Jules's work in the loos before school tomorrow morning. She won't mind, seeing as it's an emergency.

Oh, and fab news on the dancing side too! Mrs. Stepton came over in science and said she'll do the dance teaching for us, but because her partner works full-time she'll have to think of someone else to be the man. She's going to organize a couple of slots in the timetable soon so it looks like we'll get off PE for it too — how cool is that?!

At home after school on Wednesday

Newsflash!
Jules has got a date!

After English it was last break and Mr. Wright went to the staffroom and 'cos it's our actual form room we stayed put to get our coats on and that. Cosmo was getting his stuff out of his locker and me and Tilda were trying to get Jules to ask him to the prom, and Jules was going, "No! I'm too embarrassed," in a hissing whisper, and we were going, "He probably does fancy you," and "You never know until you ask," and that, but she still wouldn't and then this girl Samera came in who's in 9P and went straight up to him and said, "Will you go to the prom with Miranda?" and at first Jules was just staring at them with her eyes goggling out and then suddenly she leaped off the desk and ran over and said to him, "No, you can't 'cos you're going with me."

Everyone else in the room went completely silent and was staring at her and she looked like a *Rabbit Caught In The Headlights* as Mum calls it. Me and Tilda both had our fingers crossed and our breaths held.

Cosmo said, "But you haven't asked me," but then Jules said, "I don't *have* to ask you 'cos I'm telling you," and me and Tilda were both thinking YIKES!!! 'cos Jules can be v. v. scary sometimes. But luckily Cosmo went, "Okay, well, I suppose I'll have to then, won't I?"

So Samera shrugged and went off, and Cosmo went out to break and Jules came back over and Tilda went, "That was amazing! You were *sooooo* brave!" and Jules showed us her hands which were shaking like a leaf, no, hang on, like leaves, or like branches with leaves on in the wind, if you imagine the leaves being like her fingers. Anyway, you get what I mean – she said she'd felt really scared he'd say no but she knew she'd lose her chance if she didn't just go for it, so she gathered up all her courage! Go Jules!

It was so cool then 'cos Jules was like, "Hey, girls, thanks for our talk yesterday, it gave me that extra bit of confidence I needed!"

Tilda said, "Glad it helped," and I added, "Yeah, that's what BFF are for," and then we all three had a big squealy BFF hug. But afterwards I had a Horrible Realization, which is that Tilda and Jules have now both got someone to go to the prom with and I haven't.

EEEEEEKKKKKK!!! I'll have to do something about that – and fast! I know, I'll stop organizing for 5 mins tomorrow and have a proper think about the boys who J and T reckon fancy me, and see if I fancy any boys myself, and then I can maybe find someone to go with.

It would in fact be quite fun to go with Simon

Driscott 'cos at least we have stuff to talk about in real life, but he is only a sort of friend and not a *boy* boy, if you get what I mean, so I can't go with him really 'cos it wouldn't count as a date.

Actually, talking of Simon, he got back to me about the DJ today and he has managed to organize this person, DJ Dekz, who sounds really good, and has a cool light show and stuff. He is coming in on Thursday to meet Mr. Wright and SD so that they can check him out. I'll try and make it to that too.

So that is one more thing sorted out (hopefully!) and a big **TICK** for music organizing. Then me and Simon had this weird conversation that I did not entirely get. I will write it out the exact way I remember it, in case *you* can get what he was on about.

Simon: Lucy, I'm not sure how to say this…
well, erm, have you ever wondered why
I always agree to help you with your

	projects even though I am not remotely interested in fashion or socializing?
Me:	Yeah, sure. It's 'cos you're a technologicality geek, I mean, erm, *genius*.
Simon:	Well, I suppose I am something of a tech-head, but—
Me:	I know it's not *just* that. It's because we're sort of friends with no fancying going on whatsoever. But anyway, what were you on about that for?
Simon (looking weird like he had eaten a dodgy prawn and was about to be sick):	No reason.

So I was like, *laters*, and I walked off, but I just happened to turn around a few seconds afterwards and I saw the strange sight of Simon banging his head against the wall. I called out, "Are you okay?" thinking what if the dodgy prawn had sent him a bit crazy and he needed to go to

89

casualty, or at least the school nurse, but he just went, "I'm fine. I just slipped. I appear to have worn away the grips on my shoes without noticing. I really must complain about how slippery the cleaners make this floor! It could be extremely dangerous. There's probably some health and safety legislation about it..." and then he raced off, muttering to himself.

See what I mean about weird? I'm sure he didn't really slip. But why would he say he did when he didn't? I *soooooo* don't get what he's going on about half the time. Or actually even about 56% or maybe 61% of the time.

Just to quickly give you an update on the prom organizing, we went to see Mrs. Searle in the art room and as well as getting the classes in our year to help make decorations in art for the next couple of weeks, she reckons she can get us a red carpet — well, enough red felt to make a red carpet anyway! Plus she had the idea of asking someone in her A-level photography group to come and take pictures at the prom. She showed us their work at lunchtime and it was *sooooo* cool to be allowed in the art room when everyone else had to be outside! Some of the pix were really way out, like of just the top of someone's head with the face missing or just a hand or something, and some were really gothy, like graveyards and people moshing in dingy nightclubs (which Jules obviously liked!) but there was this set of photos by one girl called Suki which were really colourful and friendly and a bit fashiony, like girls in cool make-up in a flower bed and things like that. So Mrs. Searle is asking her if she will take the prom pictures for us. Fingers crossed she says yes!

We still need to sort out the flowers, though, 'cos after school me, Jules and Tilda went into town to the florist. The really nice girl in Blooming Marvellous showed us these displays of lovely lilies and, erm, well I'm not sure what they're called exactly, but these gorgeous purple flowers, like and some white and orange ones. It was so much fun and we felt really cool and grown-up, but we had to really control ourselves not to look massively shocked when she said the prices. We're thinking we'll have to just have one big display when you come in, rather than having flowers all up the pillars and on the buffet tables, and still it is going to be about £100 when we have zilchio money.

Oh, gotta go. I'm off to Nan's (whoops, I mean, Delia's!) to start working on my dress.

8.36 p.m.

Back from Nan's.

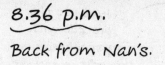

$\mathcal{I}$ have just got back from Nan's. Duh, obviously! Sorry, you could probably tell that from the heading! I am just so excited I'm not concentrating properly!

Nan has bought the material for my dress and together we made the pattern and she helped me cut out the fabric (I was way too scared to do it completely on my own in case I made a Fatal Error with the scissors, but Nan held the material flat for me so it was okay). Then she pinned it together and even though the beaded bit isn't on it yet I'm starting to get an idea of how it's going to look, which is a-*mazing*. This is it so far

93

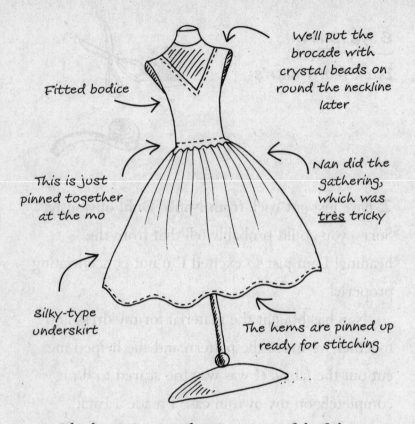

We'll put the brocade with crystal beads on round the neckline later

Fitted bodice

This is just pinned together at the mo

Nan did the gathering, which was _très_ tricky

Silky-type underskirt

The hems are pinned up ready for stitching

I had to try it on (being v. v. careful of the pins – yikes!) and while Nan was adjusting it and measuring different bits I was just looking at myself in the full-length mirror and my knees were going trembly with excitement. Then we put the dress on the dummy so we could work on it without me getting stabbed all the time, and I just couldn't stop staring at it. It's so cool to be making my own prom dress! I can't believe I'm actually doing it — it's definitely my hardest fashion challenge so far, 'cos I have to get all the lines and angles of the fabric to work so that it moves in a swishy-swishy way, which will look fab when I'm dancing. I have brought it home to do all the sewing up and hemming myself in the next week.

Thursday

and I am having the most fantastically fabulous day!

We had art this morning and we made the decorations that I'd shown Mrs. Searle in my *Crafty Things to Make and Do* book, plus some of these ones me, Jules and Tilda designed ourselves, which are like:

And we're doing these silvery, streamery thingies, like:

We are also having bunches of silver and purple balloons with long purple and silver ribbons on. Dad's hiring a helium balloon-blower-upper for us so they'll float around by the ceiling. Suki dropped in on our lesson (it must be so cool in the sixth form when you get free time and organize your own work more – the teachers should *soooooo* let *us* do that too!) and she's really keen on doing the pix for the prom. Plus I saw the DJ with Simon at first break and he gave us a demo on these decks that were in a kind of suitcase thing. We all agreed he was fab, even Mr. Wright, so we said definitely yes about him DJing at the prom, so that is something else sorted. Also, we've got our first ballroom-dancing lesson this afternoon in the hall (which means getting out of hockey in the rain – yay!). Now, if we can just work out how to get some free flowers, everything will be perfect. *SQUEAL!!!* This prom is going to be *soooooo* fantastic!

At home in a
pit of despair
Everything is boo hiss!!!

I can't believe that a few hours ago our biggest prom problem was how to get free flowers. I have written this letter to **Hey Girls!** mag for their problem page called Ask Becca, and I'm sticking it in here for safety until I can get an envelope and stamp and stuff.

Dear Ask Becca,

I know that you normally only print letters of up to 100 words so this one will be way too long, but I'm sure that when you read it and see just how serious my Reader's Problem actually <u>is</u>, you will make a whole new page for it – maybe even a Special Feature called <u>Lucy Jessica Hartley's Highly Serious Problem Special Feature</u> or something. I am going to do some pictures too, to illustrate the full problemicity, which you can use in the Special Feature if you want.

Well, first I have to quickly tell you that me and my two BFF, Jules and Tilda, are organizing our school prom. In it we are having ballroom dancing and today was our first lesson of learning it. Jules and Tilda have already got dates for the prom (Cosmo and Sanjit) so they were dancing with them and when people were pairing up for the lesson I just happened to be near Simon Driscott, who is my sort of friend with no fancying going on whatsoever, so we ended up dancing together. I still have to find a proper actual <u>boy</u>-type boy to be my date for the prom though, but that is another problem.

Back at <u>this</u> problem, we started the lesson... Oh, hang on, I should just mention that Mrs. Stepton our science teacher was teaching the ballroom dancing to us and also that we were getting off games for it. The boys were a bit annoyed about that 'cos of missing football but that is not my Highly Serious Problem. (I wish it was that simple!)

So anyway, Mrs. Stepton was teaching us and we were all going round and round the hall learning the basic steps of a waltz and then a cha-cha-cha (I know, weird name or what?!) and it was quite fun and weirdly Simon Driscott turned out to be a really good dancer. The reason I say weirdly is 'cos at this after-show party a while ago I ended up dancing with him and he was v. v. robot-ish and non-rhythmicalistic. I went, "Have you been secretly taking dancing lessons or something?" and he made a strange gurgling noise like he was choking on a Brussels sprout and went, "Of course I haven't, what a ridiculous notion, Lucy!"

BTW, I should also mention that Mrs. Stepton normally wears these kind of sandals → but that she

brought in some high heels for the dancing, which was a surprise. The high heels made her look not very teachery and she also <u>acted</u> not very teachery 'cos she let us have fun in the lesson. The boys soon cheered up 'cos they were playing human dodgems by crashing the girls into each other, like:

and then Cosmo started showing off his break-dancing and going, "I know, Miss, how about if Jules could just stand there and look hot while I go—"

I don't know what that is in fact called, so I have done a picture. It is some sort of whirling half on his head and shoulders thing with his feet in the air

Jules wasn't very keen on that un-feministic suggestion and once Cosmo was upright again she held tightly onto him so he had to do the proper steps and not the head-spinning stuff.

Mrs. Stepton said that to get us all practising hard she'd have a dance competition on the prom night and the winning boy and girl will get free tickets to Splash World and a free burger at the Cool Cats café. Well, that got everyone extra-enthusiastic and when me and Simon waltzed near to her I said a big thank you to her for helping make the prom even more fun, and she said, "You're most welcome."

The Geeky Minions were the only ones who wouldn't dance in the end (BTW, by the GMs, I mean Simon Driscott's computer-club friends. Their lives are devoted to following him around and laughing at his weird jokes and they haven't hardly even <u>talked</u> to girls before!). They were all sniggering nervously in a corner and it was like they were magnetically attached to each other 'cos every time Mrs.

Stepton tried to peel one off, another one got back into the pack. The girls from Extended Maths Club who were supposed to be dancing with them got fed up in the end and paired up with each other instead.

Sorry I have not got round to the total <u>crisis</u> bit of this letter yet, but I wanted to fill you in on the whole situation so you get how totally TERRIBLE it was when the thing that happened happened. Okay, here it is - halfway through, just when people were getting the hang of it and less toes were being stood on, Mrs. Stepton said, "Oh, just to let you know, I've asked someone to help us but he wasn't free until this period." Of course, me and Jules and Tilda were too busy trying not to laugh at her saying <u>period</u> to quite gather what she was saying but then Mr. Cain walked in and my heart totally sank through my body and down into my right foot. Well, that's what it felt like anyway.

Just so you know, Mr. Cain is my arch nemesis 'cos of him being the School Uniform Police and 'cos of me being a Style Guru. He is always getting annoyed with me about my bits of accidental nail polish and if I just have a studded belt over my skirt or whatever.

In fact, he is a total fun stopper, like

This is him sucking all the fun out of the room

Plus, he was committing crimes against fashion by wearing a too-tight ballroom dancing suit with shiny black patenty shoes and his hair all gelled back. And then of course he started acting in his sergeant-majory stricty way and taking over.

Honestly, it was awful. He kept yelling, "One, two, three!" at us and forcing us to go over the same boring steps millions of times just because one of the boys put their foot at the wrong angle or something and once simply because Cosmo smiled when we were supposed to be looking serious.

From then on it was completely awful and boring. Mr. Cain made us go round and round for the rest of the lesson doing the same steps with straight backs and no talking and <u>definitely</u> no break-dancing. Mrs. Stepton did try to take

charge again a couple
of times by suggesting we begin
some of the other dances, but he just
sort of pretended not to hear her. Then
I was struck by a thought that filled me
with Utter Horrification, which was,

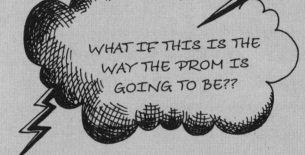

WHAT IF THIS IS THE
WAY THE PROM IS
GOING TO BE??

Luckily Simon Driscott has got a good
ballroom hold 'cos he was pretty much holding
me _up_ as I shuffled round feeling completely sick.
Argh! We've worked so hard on this prom I
can't believe it might all be ruined just by
stricty Mr. Cain!

Afterwards, when the bell went for break and the torture was over, Chantelle and Emily Jackson said to me how they had thought the prom would be fun but how they now wished they had the disco back. And some other people heard them and went, "Yeah, me too," and stuff like that and said how lame the prom will be.

I felt tears coming into my eyes but I blinked them back and managed not to cry, partly because I am a Tough Cookie who does not just crumble into a pile of chocolate chips and, erm, crumbs at the first sign of trouble, but also because Mr. Cain was there and if I'd started crying he would have noticed that I was wearing Ultra Lash Volumizing Mascara in Jet Midnight, as there would have been streaks of it running down my face, and I would have got detention because it is meant to be No Make-Up. I couldn't even say anything 'cos then he

shushed us all and
made us file out of the hall in silence
and even though I was psychically trying
to tell everyone It's not my fault by the
power of telepathy, I don't think they got
the message and I felt so embarrassed
I wanted the hall floor to open up and
swallow me, especially as the girls loos are
right underneath so I would just drop down
into a cubicle where I could flush myself down
the toilet and never be seen again.

Argh! and Double argh!

So, Ask Becca, you can see why my problem
deserves a Special Feature all to itself.

I really wish I could announce in assembly
that I had no idea Mr. Cain was teaching us, or
that I could stick posters up round the school
saying I did plan for the prom to be cool and not
geeky. I want to tell Mrs. Stepton to un-invite him
to help, but I can't 'cos she is a teacher and you

know how teachers always have to stick together, plus she might think I'm being ungrateful about her helping us, which I'm not but...

Triple argh!

Oh, I wish Mr. Cain could somehow magically not exist. I feel like the prom is going to be rubbish, and after all our hard work arranging things! So please, please, pleeeeease reply straight away and tell us how we can make Mr. Cain suddenly decide he doesn't want to help out with the prom after all. Thanks a gazillion!

Yours in massive desperateness,

Lucy Jessica Hartley

6.17 p.m.

As I quickly mentioned in my *Ask Becca*
letter, I have still got the other problem of finding
a date for the prom. Well, hopefully I have got that
sorted out now, at least. I did try, but I didn't
suddenly start fancying any of the other boys at
school today, so I suppose it is down to:

BEN JONES

STEFANO STEFANOPOLIS

DANIEL ARCHER

Ben Jones is the most okayish but I reckon Susie James fancies him too. She is this girl in our class who is sometimes really nice but who can also get totally moody with people for no reason. I don't want her to start being moody with *me* so I think I will steer myself clear of Ben.

Oh, gotta go, Mum's calling me down to tea.

22 minutes later

*B*efore tea I was just standing in the kitchen wondering how to decide between the two leftover boys and Mum was serving up dinner and suddenly I had an idea about letting Fate decide instead of me. So I went, "Mum, can I borrow two bits of spaghetti?" and she let me, so I took them out of the drainer and put one in each hand. I named them Stef and Daniel and then I threw them at the wall.

Mum screeched, "Lucy, what on earth are you doing?" and I was like, "Choosing my date for the prom, obviously."

"Oh, obviously," she said in a sarky way, and we both stood there and watched the spaghetti sticking to the wall. Just then Stef's bit fell off onto the floor, and I said, "That's settled, then, I'm going with Daniel."

Mum did her head-shaking thing which means, *Even though you are my very own daughter, Lucy, sometimes I wonder what planet you are on.*

So, I have picked a boy and I just have to ask him out (or get Jules or Tilda to do it for me, more likely!).

Friday at first break

I am sitting on the loo
(don't worry, I mean the
closed seat of the loo!)
writing this while waiting
for Jules and Tilda to
come back.

They have just gone to ask Daniel Archer to go
to the prom with me and when they get back
we're going to practise doing our red-carpet walk
up and down the loos so we look really good
entering the prom.

2 mins later

Jules and Tilda came back but now they have gone
again because annoyingly Daniel Archer is already

going to the prom with someone else. Apparently
Jules said, "But you told me you fancied Lucy,"
and Daniel just shruggingly went, "Yeah, but now
I is hangin' wid Liana Hawley, innit." Huh!
Charming! Plus, why can't boys talk normally?!
Well, I don't need someone who is that shallow,
so there! Now J and T have gone to ask Stefano
instead. Fate was obviously guiding me to choose
the boy whose spaghetti strand *fell down first*.
I just read the signs wrong.

6 mins later

Well now I have no idea what Fate is in fact doing
'cos Jules came back and said she has got bad news
and how Stef is already going with Genevieve.
Huh! Typical!

I have gone from Dating Guru to Dating Disaster in one easy move. I even checked with Ben, but he is going with Ricosha, apparently.

Argh-orama!!!

Most people have dates now and I got Tilda and Jules to check out a few more boys for me and I can officially tell you that there are **NO** boys left to choose from, apart from the Geeky Minions (and Tilda says not even *they* are available 'cos they're going as a group with the girls from her Extended Maths Club).

Seriously, not exaggerating, I am in complete and utter despair. I wish I had asked a boy to the prom sooner, or got Tilda and Jules to tell people I fancied them so they would ask *me*, but I was too busy with all the organizing stuff and making my dress and that.

117

How embarrassing to be the only girl without a date, especially when I am one of the organizers! This is what my prom photo will look like:

Cardboard cut-out of a boy

Or even worse, like this:

Friday night,

lying on my bed
feeling miserable.

Argh! After what happened today I am in Total Mortification and I am planning to never leave my bedroom ever again!

Okay, I will try to calm down and tell you the disaster of today from the beginning. After break, we all filed into the hall for the second ballroom dancing lesson and Mrs. Stepton was there but You-Know-Who was not (I don't mean Voldemort but someone way worse, i.e. Mr. Cain). So I was thinking *yessity-yes-yes he is not coming and Mrs. Stepton will just teach us on our own and it will be fun and everyone will be into it again and no one will think the prom is geeky and I will not have to go and live in a cave in Outer Mongolia 'cos of my despair* (not sure if they have caves there, but anyway, I mean somewhere really far away that has caves).

I was dancing with Simon again, at least
I thought I was, but just while I was in
distractedness, this girl Melissa grabbed his arm
and dragged him away. The reason I was in
distractedness was 'cos I had just said to Simon,
"Are you going to the prom as a group with the
Extended Maths girls and the Geeky Minions,
whoops, sorry, I mean your Charming Friends?"
He'd said no and how he was in fact not going
with anyone yet and so I went into distractedness
thinking about how:

1. Simon is already my dance partner by
   coincidence.
2. He is also a good dancer, in fact he is the best
   out of all the boys (if you don't include break-
   dancing, that is).
3. We get on really well (when he is not
   correcting my grammaticalness).
4. He is funny and makes me laugh.

5. So I should ask him to the prom 'cos even though we are just sort of friends with no fancying going on whatsoever and he is not a *boy*-type boy, at least I'll have someone to go with who is funny and interesting to talk to and a good dancer.

As you can see, that is a lot of thinking – 5 thoughts in fact – so you can understand why I was in the distractedness. Anyway, I'd definitely decided to ask him to the prom and so I went over to him. Melissa was still holding his arm and there was a group of girls round them, including Carrie from 9H who is like *the* prettiest girl in our entire year. Seriously, I am not joking, she looks like this ↗

waves of gorgeousness

121

I listened in and you would not believe what was going on. You know how Melissa totally kidnapped Simon from me against his will? Well, now they were all fighting over him! Gracie was going, "Mel, I'll swap you my Groovy Chick pencil case for him." And Melissa was like, "No way, he's mine, I bagsied him first."

I was completely confused about why they would all suddenly want Simon Driscott, but then he went, "I'm not an object, you know," and Melissa went, "Shut up, twinkletoes," and I realized it was 'cos of his ballroom dancing abilities.

Then Kasia said, "I'll give you my curl-and-twirl hair braider for him," and Melissa went, "What, including the beads and thread?" and Kasia said, "Yeah. Well, I've used up all the red but apart from that it's the complete set." I was really annoyed then, so I stepped into the circle and went, "In case you hadn't noticed, that is MY dancing partner you're on about."

"Too late, babe, I bagsied him," said Melissa, really annoyingly, so I went, "But still, *I* should have him 'cos you only like him *now* but I have been his sort of friend for ages, even though I used to think he was a Prince of Pillockdom." I gave Simon a big smile then to show our friendshipness to everyone, and I was expecting him to smile back, but for some reason he looked really evilly at me and went, "Yeah, thanks so much for that, Lucy," in a mega-ly sarcastic way. Then he turned to the kidnappers and said, "Right, ladies, no need to fight over me. I'll dance with Carrie, and take her to the prom if she wants me to."

I was in complete FLABBERGASTED GOBSMACKEDNESS that he had just asked out *the* prettiest girl in our entire *year* and I was waiting for her to say no, but then I was in GOBSMACKED FLABBERGASTATION 'cos she said YES!

I can't believe Simon Driscott picked another girl to dance with and go to the prom with when

123

he is supposed to be *my* sort of friend! And the *look* he gave me! Well, I was only standing up for him but you'd think I'd said something terrible!

And can you believe he just asked her to the prom, faster than a speeding bullet, without even *thinking* about me and who I was supposed to go with! I mean, char-*ming*!

While I was still standing there with my mouth hanging open in a state of **SHOCKED STUNNEDNESS** Carrie said to Simon, "We'd better start practising now for the prom – with your dancing we'll win the dance comp *and* I'm bound to be voted prom queen because of how pretty and popular I am! Do you think I should have my hair up or down on the night? I've got to think about which would look best with the tiara and there'll be lots of photos and…"

I didn't hear any more (thank goodness!) 'cos she had dragged him off to start practising. Huh! She'd better not win! I'd decided to save money by *making* a beautiful tiara for the prom queen. But I don't want to make one for the girl who stole **MY PARTNER**! In fact, I wish we hadn't put anything about the prom queen and king on the poster we made now, then no one would know about it and we could just cancel that bit of things!

Poor Ryan, the captain of the Year 9 football team, was just left standing there looking completely heartbroken 'cos he was supposed to be going to the prom with Carrie. I was having a total panic by then about Simon **CRUELLY ABANDONING** me and me having to go to the prom on my ownio, so I asked Ryan to be my partner and go with *me* instead.

Luckily he said yes, so I got to give Simon Driscott a smug look, at least – ha!

Unfortunately, while me and Ryan were dancing, I couldn't find one single thing in my brain to say to him, which is not a problem I normally have. The problem I normally have is shutting up long enough to breathe! But I have tried to think positive and focus on his good points, which are:

A) I have a date (phew!).

B) He is good-looking to most people (although he is not my type personally) so he will look good in any pix of us together.

C) He is okayish at dancing, apart from the fact that the turns are like being tackled on the footie pitch and also he trod on 3 of my toes.

But at the moment his good points are outweighed by one big bad point:

His personality is so different from mine we are like this:

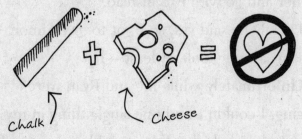

Chalk

Cheese

When the okayish boys like Jamie Cousins and that saw who Simon was dancing with, they all started doing stupid boys' stuff like high-fiving and weird handshakes that Simon Driscott didn't know how to do at first, and going, "Nice one, mate, Carrie's well fit!" as if they come from the East End of London instead of the fields of Dorset. Simon was acting like he thought they were being a bit silly but I could tell he was secretly pleased about the boys thinking he is cool.

Then Mr. Cain turned up (*boo hiss!!*) and of course it all became strict and boring again.

As they passed us, Jules and Tilda were both doing looks at me meaning *Well done!* and *Good choice!* about Ryan, but I don't feel like I have done well. Whenever we passed Carrie and Simon he seemed to be making her laugh and then once when Mr. Cain stopped us all to show us this step again, that according to him we were, "Just not getting because you are not applying the appropriate level of effort to the task" (see what I mean about him making it *yawn-oramic?*), Carrie started touching SD's hair and putting it in a different style, until Mr. Cain said, "Leave Mr.

Driscott alone, Miss Love." Suddenly my brain started thinking, *Yeah, don't touch his hair!* Not that I am remotely bothered about Simon Driscott's hair normally but for some reason it made me really annoyed.

Then when I thought things couldn't get any worser than worse, Mr. Cain said, "While I have never attended the 'disco', I do think this 'prom' will be excellent. I intend to come along and ensure that you're all getting the steps right. Well done, Lucy, Julietta and Matilda-Jane for organizing this."

It's the first time Mr. Cain has ever said "Well done" to me in my entire life but I was completely wishing he hadn't. He started a clap for us and everyone had to join in but they did it not-very-enthusiastically and they were giving me annoyed looks – as if I *meant* for the prom to be a swotty thing that Mr. Cain likes!

Argh! And he's even told Simon we won't need any disco lights because he wants the room to be very brightly lit so he can supervise the dancing properly. Everyone is going to hate the prom SO much and the whole thing is going to be AWFUL!

Even worse, no one is ever going to forget about this, and they are going to blame us for this rubbish boring event for EVER! I can't believe he's ruined our prom just like that! After all our effort! My life has turned into a complete NIGHTMARE!

11.04 p.m.

I just now went downstairs 'cos I couldn't sleep. (Hmmm, I wonder why not? Maybe 'cos my life has become a total disaster zone!) Mum was just about to say she was having No Nonsense and send me back to bed but my face must have looked mega-ly sad 'cos instead she said, "Why don't I make us some hot chocolate and you can tell me all about it?"

So I told her about Mr. Cain wrecking the ballroom dancing lessons and maybe even the prom as well after all our hard work.

Mum had put one marshmallow in my hot chocolate but when she heard my Tale Of Woe she got the packet down again and gave me two more. "That man!" she exclaimed. "I have no idea why he went into teaching, I really don't!" (BTW, she doesn't like him after he was evilly mean to me for

130

just simply setting up a secret Style School at lunchtimes in the loos.)

But she couldn't think of any way to help us.

I *have* to think of some way to get rid of him…and fast! Mum says I should sleep on it because sometimes if you go to sleep with a big problem buzzing round your brain you wake up with an ingenious solution. But I don't have time to do that – I have to start trying to think of a solution right *now*, even if it takes all night and I have to hold my eyes actually open so I don't fall asleep and so I can write my idea straight away in here if I get one.

Yawn

It has been 18 minutes and still no ideas. Actually maybe I will do the thinking with my eyes closed and the light off instead of writing it down

Saturday

yessity yes yes!
Mum was right – it worked!

Well, as you can probably tell from the squiggly end to my writing last night, I did end up (accidentally!) sleeping on my Mr. Cain problem and I've just had probably the most brilliant *Creative Inspiration* of all the *Creative Inspirations* I have ever had in my entire life!!

So I straight away rang Jules and went, "Hey, Jules, your mum and dad could come and teach cool Latin dances to everyone for the prom!"

"Terrible idea!" Jules grumbled (I think she had just woken up).

"Jules, please believe me, they are fab!" I cried. "With their help, we could get rid of Mr. Cain and make the prom brilliant again!"

"Humph," went Jules, still not sounding very convinced, but she agreed to ask them, seeing as it was for the Bigger Picture of saving the prom. And also because we had zero other ideas. So she left me dangling on the phone and about 4 heart-stoppingly tense minutes later she came back on and said they said **YES**! So then I rang Tilda, who thought it was a fab idea straight away!

So on Monday morning us three **BFF** are going to go and explain to Mrs. Stepton that Jules's parents are coming to help in our dance lessons. We have got the good idea of saying that we have done the ballroom and now we are going on to the Latin, so we need some dancers who know about that to teach us. Hopefully (fingers crossed) she will get the hint and realize that we are trying to get rid of Mr. Cain. I really hope she won't be upset and think we are trying to get rid of her as well. And I really *really* hope our plan works – I think it's our only chance of saving the prom!

Right, I have to get ready now 'cos I am working on my dress absolutely all day so Nan can check it when I see her on Monday night.

Sunday

Dad is coming to take us out today but first he's having a lie-in 'cos apparently he was v. busy yesterday with paperwork and then he had to go in to the radio station to do his Saturday night show, so now he is v. v. tired. Actually, Mum told me that Jules's mum Isabella told her that Dad went round their house after his show and sat up drinking brandy with Jules's dad while playing their guitars until 5 o'clock in the morning, so *that* is in fact why he is tired. I don't mind though, because I need the extra time to design the tiara for the prom queen (who had better not be Carrie!).

I reckon the boy who will be king will be too embarrassed to wear a crown so I am not going to even bother making one. Mum is going to get me a big bar of Dairy Milk for him as the prize instead, 'cos she's going to the supermarket "when *your father* finally crawls out of his pit and comes round here to fulfil his parental duties like a responsible adult" (*her* words, obviously!).

She also said to me and Alex, "I know you won't have a proper meal out with *your father*, so what do you fancy for tea?" and Alex said lasagne so that's what we're having. Since they split up, Mum mainly calls Dad *your father* instead of Brian, which she used to call him. But at least she didn't sound too annoyed with him for being late or not ever giving us salads, and only said it in a rolling-her-eyes-and-going-"Tut! Typical!" sort of way. She always hides loads of peppers and spinach in the lasagne anyway, so we will get our vitamins. That is our secret from Alex, though, 'cos he wouldn't eat it if he knew, so *shhhhh!*

<u>12.30-ish</u>

Here is my tiara design for the prom queen.

I am making it from some of the wire that Dad left in the garage, and some beads and jewels from my stash of bits and pieces. Some are from the craft shop but mainly I buy old necklaces and bracelets from charity shops and then chop them up and reuse the beads.

Oh, that's the doorbell – Dad's here at last.

136

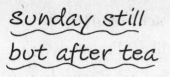

Sunday still but after tea

Dad took us to the cinema to see the new Harry Potter movie and it was *soooooo* cool. It was especially good 'cos he had a bit of a headache, so to get some Peace and Quiet, he let us have popcorn and sweets and a drink each instead of making us share (which always leads to a loud argument because of Alex's immaturity).

Talking of my little brother, he changed straight into his Harry Potter costume when he got home and he is now busy running round the house trying to turn things into other things with his wand. He is *soooooo* obsessed with HP that he keeps bumping into things and telling Mum he needs glasses like Harry's, but obviously she's not falling for *that* again after taking him to the optician's last month. Plus, he reckons he is not coming to Tambridge High next year, but that instead he will be getting a letter from Hogwarts.

When he said that, I was like, "I'm sorry to inform you that Hogwarts is not a real school and is only in a book," but he just did a Knowing Look at me and said, "That's exactly what we *want* you muggles to think," and then he went into pretending he was in a wizarding duel so I had to edge past him to get up the stairs to the peacefulness of my room so I could write in here and also carry on putting the beads on the brocade-y bit for the top of my dress.

Which I am going to do now.

So *bye!*

Monday

I am just quickly writing this in the loos.

This morning we asked Mrs. Stepton about having Jules's parents in to teach the Latin dancing and she said that's fine so we are All Systems Go. She didn't say she would tell Mr. Cain not to come, though, but fingers crossed she has got the hint and just isn't letting us *know* that she has got the hint because of her professionalistic teacheriness.

Oh, speaking of Mrs. Stepton, she has just come in here and now she is chucking us out of the loos into the playground for our Fresh Air and Exercise. I'll just flush the toilet so it looks like I was really using it for actually going to the loo!

139

The time is NOW
Ha ha!

I have just been at Nan's sewing the beaded brocade-y bit onto my dress, and getting her to check what I've done so far. When I put it on it was the Moment Of Truth and my heart was pounding in case I'd somehow got the stitching all wrong and it didn't fit — but luckily it did and it looked *fabulicious*, even when it was just plain before we sewed the sparkly bit on. We did have to unpick this one seam I did a bit wonky, though, but Nan said I'd done a really good job and that she thinks I'll be cutting couture gowns in no time. Fingers crossed I will, seeing as my life's ambition is to be a *Real Actual Fashion Designer*!

The dress is coming together really well. This is where we are with it so far.

All the stitching is done

The sash and bow will go here

Now we've added the gorgeous top layer

We put an extra layer of net stuff under in the end, so it sticks out more

I have brought it home again to sew on the waist bow. Then on Thursday we'll have the final fitting and Nan will check over everything I've done and make sure it's not going to suddenly fall apart in front of everyone or anything (which would be *sooooo* embarrassing!).

Oh, gotta go, my bath's run. I'm going to use loads of Mum's relaxational bubble bath 'cos there's so much going on with the prom organizing and my dress and the dancing and stuff, my head is in a whirl and I *soooooo* need it!

in the loos at lunchtime.

Hooray! We have solved our dance teacher problem! Lucky I didn't get round to sending my *Ask Becca* letter!

At first when we all went into the hall my heart sank right into the bottom of my special-occasion high heels (which I had persuaded Mum to let me take to school to wear for the dancing lesson). To be ready, I changed into them as soon as I arrived and then I forgot to take them off afterwards, and so I sort of ended up wearing them all morning. It was so cool 'cos even these two sixth-formers said how fab they looked and I felt like a fashion diva.

Anyway, going back to the point, my heart was sinking into my fab shoes, not 'cos Jules's mum and dad weren't there (because they were), but because Mr. Cain *was* there (when I was praying he wouldn't be).

We got into our pairs and Mrs. Stepton introduced Isabella and Gabriel and they started showing us the basic steps to this cool dance called the salsa, but then Mr. Cain started trying to take over, even though he didn't know absolutely anything about it. Like, if anyone even just coughed he started pointing at them and going, "You, boy, don't be so rude to our guests!" in his most stricty voice. It was making everyone get very bored and annoyed, and me, Jules and Tilda were freaking out thinking that he was going to ruin our plans **AGAIN** when luckily Gabriel, Jules's dad, just went, "Why don't you have a try, Mr. Cain?" and before he could reply Jules's mum grabbed him in a strong hold more like a wrestler than a dancer and everyone started smiling except Jules, who tried to shuffle behind one of the curtains and quietly **DIE** of mortification.

Gabriel changed the music to a tango and everyone watched as Isabella dragged Mr. Cain round the floor. She was saying stuff like, "Let

yourself go! Feel the passion! Look into my eyes!
Find your inner *toro*!" and she kept letting out
these whoops like "AIIIIII!" that made him jump.
He was so tense he was like an ironing board going
round and even Ryan looked like a fab dancer
compared to him. When the music finished,
Isabella wrapped one of her legs round Mr. Cain's
knee and threw herself backwards so her spine was
almost bent completely in half for the finale, like:

It was SOOOOOO funny to see Mr. Cain in total embarrassment, I *soooooo* wish you went to my school so you could have seen it. Everyone was staring with their eyes popping out and nearly bursting into giggles. Then we all started clapping, and doing the whooping "AIIIII!!!" sounds and Mr. Cain couldn't tell us off 'cos a guest was doing them first!

He was SO completely bright red and puffed out he couldn't even say anything for ages. His mouth was just opening and shutting and I know inside he was completely freaking out, because a bit of hair from his perfect side-parting fell forwards and he didn't even bother to put it back in its place.

"Well, I, that's most interesting," he stammered at last. "Erm, I'm sure you've got it under control and I can leave Mrs. Stepton to supervise because I've just remembered I've got some Year 11s in detention tonight and I need to prepare for, yes, um…"

Well, he said something like that, I couldn't really hear because he was more like mumbling it than saying it, and then, seriously I am not exaggerating, he **BOLTED** out of the hall.

As soon as the doors closed behind him everyone started clapping and whooping again and Jules came out from behind the curtain and was staring in amazement 'cos the people around us were saying how cool her mum and dad are and how they have saved us from Mr. Cain. I knew Mrs. Stepton wanted to join in the celebration too, but being teachery she just had to look disapproving and make us be quiet and settle down.

So everything is cool again and Isabella and Gabriel were **ABSOLUTELY AMAZING** and they have made everyone keen on the dancing and now no one thinks the prom will be rubbish and no one is doing whispering about me in the lunch hall — so *YAY!*

We are learning the jive, the tango and the salsa. And they are helping Mrs. Stepton go over the waltz with us too, although we will probably never forget it after Mr. Cain made us do it about 1,000 times!

I can't remember what you call the moves you do in the different dances, so I have made up my own names for them:

The girly-twirly-whirly

The toe-tapper

The standing on hot coals

The spin the girl round your head ~~maneuver~~ ~~maneuvre~~ maneuvere

Oh, never mind about the spelling, you get what I mean!

Okay, okay, so I made that last one up entirely, but it *was* nearly true 'cos the boys were getting really overenthusiastic about the spins and sort of competing with each other, going, "Hey, look, if you pull her arm like this she whizzes round really fast." So there were lots of dizzy girls, but at least the boys were doing the ballroom instead of just wanting to break-dance.

At the end, Isabella and Gabriel got us all to do a clap for each other and said to keep practising between lessons if we want a chance of winning

Mrs. Stepton's dance comp prize on the night. *Not* that there's any way I'm going to win even if me and Ryan do a gazillion hours of rehearsing. Dancing with that boy is like hauling a plank of wood around the room while trying to stop it from breaking your foot bones.

Tilda is doing well with Sanjit, though, and they might even have a chance of beating the annoyingly good Carrie and Simon Driscott (i.e. the boy who should be MY partner if she hadn't stolen him!). Jules is doing okayish with Cosmo except that Isabella keeps telling her the *man* is supposed to lead. Of course, Jules being Jules is not having any of that, and especially not off her own *mum*, so her and Cosmo carried on arguing about who had to go more backwards for the rest of the lesson.

Oh, speaking of Jules, she has just come in here (*oooooh*, spooky, maybe I really am turning psychic!) and we are going to go on the field and practise our dance steps.

MORE GREAT NEWS!!!

(This might be my
ACTUAL Lucky Day!!!)

Suki our sixth former photography star went to
Blooming Marvellous the florist to look at some
flowers for her next set of pictures and she showed
the lady the ones she's done already…and the lady
liked them so much she says if Suki will do one
of her little boy in some flowers she will give her
a big arrangement for free! So anyway, Suki came
up to me at break and she was like, "Have you
ordered the flowers for your prom yet?" and I was
like, "No, 'cos we can't afford any," and she was
like, "No problem, 'cos you can have my
arrangement I'm getting for free." I was going,
"Are you sure?" and all that stuff you have to say
because of politeness, even when you really want
to go, "Yes, we do want them!" straight away. She
said she definitely is sure 'cos having nice flowers

will make the prom photos look better which will be good for her too 'cos she might put a few in her portfolio.

How brilliant is that?! Suki is amazing!

We had another meeting with Mr. Phillips today to run through everything, and he is really happy with what we've done on the prom organizing so far. He was so happy in fact that I thought he might actually get Debbie his secretary to make me a coffee if I asked for one but I didn't quite dare!

I had a meeting with Simon Driscott as well to go over the lighting and sound stuff and he has everything under control, so that's cool. I know he **CRUELLY ABANDONED** me for Carrie but I am staying professionalistic for the sake of the prom, i.e. I only talked about businessy stuff and not normal sort-of-friend-type stuff, and I only accidentally-on-purpose trapped his hand between the desks once (well, okay, it was twice). The Geeky Minions, whoops, I mean, his Charming Friends, are helping him set up the lights and that after school tomorrow in the hall, with Mr. Wright supervising so they don't go climbing up poles that they aren't supposed to and that kind of thing. Plus, we went to the art room and Mrs. Searle showed us all the decorations the art classes have made for the prom and they look completely fab! In fact we were so busy today with prom meetings that we felt really professionalistic and it was hardly like school at all, apart from lessons getting in the way, of course.

I'm going to get my accessories box out now and work out which necklace and bracelets and earrings and that I'm going to wear to the prom with my dress, and I'm also going to have an experiment with my hair 'cos it would be cool to have it in a wavy style with clips in and these little butterflies I recently got from New Look instead of it just hanging there boringly like normal. I want to look so amazingly different and grown-up and fab that girls hardly recognize me and are going, "Is that really Lucy Jessica Hartley? I just thought for a minute that it was a top model or a Real Actual Fashion Designer 'cos she looks so cool," and the boys are silently staring at me with their eyeballs popping out of their heads and their mouths doing that hanging open thing I was mentioning before (*and* Simon Driscott is really massively sorry he ditched me for Carrie and **CRUELLY ABANDONED** me to dance with Ryan the plank of wood).

Not that I'm even bothered about what SD thinks any more, but anyway.

Thursday

only 2 days till the prom!

I am just writing in here to say sorry I don't have time to write in here. Oh whoops, I already have by writing that!

So I'll also quickly tell you that we had another dancing lesson today with Isabella and Gabriel. They said we are shaping up nicely and it was really fun too so that was cool! Me and Ryan even got the step I call the girly-twirly-whirly right, at last, so he is not being *completely* useless.

And finally, I just wanted to write something down in here that was really kind of *wow* so I don't forget it and so that when I am massively old, like about 25 or something, I can read it back and remember this most amazing feeling. Tonight I was at Nan's and together we put the finishing touches on the dress and she helped me into it and I stood in front of the mirror and she stood behind me and fussed about with it a bit and I was adjusting the front and going, "I just can't believe I've made my own prom dress, it's the hardest designing challenge I've ever had," and thanking her for helping me. Then suddenly we both just stopped and stared into the mirror and Nan put her hands on my shoulders and it was like, well, I just felt so grown-up and also like I have this whole exciting life ahead of me that is really only just starting. I'm not explaining it very well, but I hope you can get what I mean anyway. I really think Nan was feeling the same, 'cos she gave me a smile that sort of said so without her using actual words (I really, really think I am turning psychic after that!).

Plus, even though they are still no way near as big as J and T's, my you-know-whats have actually got a bit bigger recently so I look even better in the dress than I thought I would!

Friday

Prom Day tomorrow – yippeeeeee!!!

I am still massively busy with all the prom prep, but just to say that Mrs. Searle let us bring down the decorations from the art room to the hall after school and they are ready to put up tomorrow. Mrs. Searle and Mrs. Stepton are coming to help us tomorrow too, which is very nice of them seeing as it is their day off from having to see any Very Actual Teenagers.

Gladys and Beryl have done most of the food and put it on these big serving platter things that look silver but are actually made out of really solid tinfoil stuff, and they are coming in at 10 a.m. tomorrow as well to finish off the final touches. They have got us the fruit juices we asked for and me and Jules and Tilda are going to make our cocktails when we arrive in school tomorrow

158

morning. Gladys even managed to get the cherries and umbrellas we wanted from a catering catalogue so they weren't too expensive after all. That's so cool and it will make them look amazing.

I can't wait!!!!

Saturday the 19th of November

Prom Day!

While Mum is painting my toenails with Candyfloss Pink I just want to say *Yippeeeeee!!!!!!* it is finally Prom Day! It is 4 — hang on while I check — 4.16 p.m. and me, Jules and Tilda are round mine getting ourselves ready for the prom and Mum is helping us.

This morning we went to the school (it was really weird being there on a Saturday, not in our uniforms and with no one else there) and we got everything ready with help from Mrs. Searle and Mrs. Stepton and Gladys and Beryl. I took in the box I made for the prom queen and king nominations, which used to be a shoebox, but now looks like this —

Everyone's going to have one vote for the
prom queen and one for the king, and DJ Dekz
is going to tell everyone to pick the people they
think best reflect the spirit of the prom, so
maybe the ones who've put the most into their
dancing and clothes and that, or the ones who are
having loads of fun and making it go with a swing.
We're putting the box on the table just before the
food, so you can quickly write your vote as you're
lining up. Tilda thought of that good organizing
idea, of course! Gladys and Beryl are going to do
the vote counting, 'cos they have to be there to
put more food out anyway, so that's good, 'cos

A) I would rather be dancing and having fun than counting bits of paper

and

B) maths is not exactly my best subject so I would probably count it wrong anyway.

I am going to announce the winners with the DJ's mike and award the tiara and chocolate though, so I have to look extra nice 'cos I'll be standing on the stage and absolutely everyone will see me.

Oh hang on, Mum wants to do my fingernails now so writing will become a bit tricky. I'll just be a sec…

6 mins later

Hi again! I think they're dry enough now — I have been blowing on them to speed them up. I have

also got a face pack on and so have Jules and Tilda.
Here's a quick pic of us:

This is me writing in
here to you – hello!!!

Hee hee! Jules just said to Tilda, "You are
going to look so nice...for Sanjit!" and Tilda
blushed so much you could even almost see her
cheeks go red under the face pack and that set us
all off giggling.

Gotta go, Mum's going to do our make-up now so we have to run upstairs and wash the face packs off. She's put everything out on the kitchen table and lined the chairs up like in a proper beauty parlour and put out her old *Celeb* mags for us to read while we're waiting to be done. Cool or what?! I'm so glad Mum's a make-up artist – it's much more useful than, say, being a kilt-maker or a cheese taster – well, unless we needed kilts or special cheese, I suppose, which isn't that likely.

Oh, I just can't **WAIT** for tonight! Please wish me luck for everything going well 'cos it's most likely the last chance I'll have to write in here.

Really gotta go now – Jules and Tilda are saying hurry up. And now they are pulling m

Really massively late o'clock

Soooooo much happened tonight, and it was—
No, hang on, I will take a deep breath and start
from where I left off 'cos I don't want to miss
anything out. BTW, Tilda and Jules stayed over
after the prom and we were all whispering for ages
but they are asleep now. I thought I'd be able to
get to sleep the second we finally stopped talking
(after saying goodnight for the gazillionth time
and then one of us speaking again!) but I ended
up just lying here thinking of everything that has
happened – and grinning!

Right, here goes. When Mum had done our
make-up and hair we went upstairs to change. Mr.
Van der Zwan arrived while we were up there and
so did Dad, and when we came down in our
dresses they took loads of photos so it felt like we
were film stars being snapped by the ~~paparatsi~~

~~papparrazi~~ oh, it is way too late at night to be bothered with spelling – I mean those newspaper people with cameras who stalk celebs! Mr. Van der Zwan got Tilda to do a turn in the kitchen and he said, "You look so beautiful, and so grown-up," with his voice going all wobbly.

So you can see that under all his Stricty Dadness he is quite a softy after all. Plus, he was right, because Tilda looked a-*mazing* with her hair all shiny and done up in curls and the lovely Star-Shimmer eyeshadow Mum had put on her. Then he said how lovely me and Jules looked too. In fact, here is a pic of what we looked like:

Dad had polished his red sports car specially for us and put the top down (cool!) and, you will never guess what…he had even bought a chauffeur's hat from a costume shop! *And* he held the door open and said, "Ladies…" for us to get in. As you can guess,  Mum was nearly fainting with the shock about his chivalrousness. Tilda's dad followed behind us in his Volvo to take some pix of us getting out at the prom, and the journey there was one of the best times **EVER** in my whole life, 'cos we felt so cool, and it lasted ages and ages too, 'cos we made Dad go really slow so the wind didn't mess up our hairstyles.

We got there and while Tilda's dad was taking pix of us, Sanjit came up. He said how lovely Tilda looked (making her blush 1 zillion watts, **BTW**) and he was just about to pin this flower thing he'd got called a corsage to her dress when Mr. Van der Zwan marched over and swiped it out of his hand

and said, "*I'll* pin that on, thank you very much."
Sanjit looked absolutely terrified and he was just
going, "Yes, sir, no, sir, yes, sir," to everything
Mr. V said, even though Mr. V is not even a
teacher. Of course, Tilda was having a gigantic
CRINGE so she quickly kissed her dad goodbye
and we all said thanks to my dad and then we
hurried into the school and then we just totally
collapsed into giggles. Well, us three **BFF** did –
Sanjit still looked petrified!

There were some people outside the hall
waiting for friends and dates and that, and Ryan
and Cosmo were there. Cosmo had a dinner suit
on, but the trousers were really low with no belt
and his bright patterny pants were totally showing
– **NOT** very sophisticated! Still, Jules didn't seem
to mind. She grabbed him by the arm and steered
him down the red carpet. Ryan looked really
heart-throbby and he said I looked nice too, and
even though that was the end of what we could
think of to say to each other, at least he will look

good in the picture we had taken on the way in, and I haven't ended up with a cardboard cut-out boy or an empty space where a boy is meant to be like I was worried about.

When we turned away from Suki the photographer and actually walked into the hall, I just stopped completely still for a moment and luckily I was holding Ryan's arm 'cos my legs had gone all trembly with wonder and amazement. Everyone looked lovely, and the girls were all in dresses, even Augusta Rinaldi and her sporty lot who never normally wear anything but tracksuit stuff. The dresses made the room look really colourful, and the silver decorations were sparkly in the spotlights and the balloons were bobbing about by the ceiling with their ribbons hanging down, and the food table looked amazing, 'cos Gladys and Beryl had put jars with bright yellow and purple flowers all along it, and scattered little silver

stars in between the platters. And best of all –
Mr. Cain wasn't there, *yippeeeeeee!!!*

Jules and Tilda were staring too – we just
couldn't believe we had had the idea and made
all this come true! Suddenly we all looked at each
other at the same time and ran over and had a
big **BFF** hug. It was another one of the best ever
moments of my life so far and I hope I will
remember it for **EVER!**

There's so much more I still want to tell you
but I can hardly keep my eyes open. I haven't even
told you the best or most amazing or most
unbelievable things that happened yet but

It is Sunday morning!

Can you believe we
all slept till 10.18?!

Now it's 2.30 p.m. and Jules and Tilda have gone
home and Dad has taken Alex to the park to play
football (I stayed here with Mum 'cos I wanted
to chill out after all the excitingness of yesterday).
I have just made myself a cup of tea and persuaded
Mum to let me have another one of her scrummy
Belgian chocolate brownies from Marks by doing
all the washing up from lunch, and now I'm going
to curl up on the sofa and carry on telling you
about the prom…

Right after I have
a big bite of this…

Yum!

Well, just after I was being speechless about
how amazing everything looked, I felt so happy,
so when I spotted Simon Driscott I went up to

say hi and I also said, "I like your hair," 'cos he had done something different with it. But instead of speaking he was just staring at me with his mouth opening and shutting like a flabbergasted goldfish, with no words coming out. At the  time, I was thinking, *How strange, maybe his bow tie is a bit tight.* I have now found out that it was because of a different reason, which I will tell you in a minute. Eventually he managed to say that Carrie had changed his hair, which I found really annoying, even though it looked way better like that.

Then Carrie came up and we fake-smiled at each other and she marched Simon off and I was watching him get her a Purple Sunrise and I felt really, well, this will sound massively weird, but *jealous.* I thought maybe it was 'cos she had stolen my dance partner, but it felt like more than that. So then I was standing there sipping the Apple Cooler Ryan handed me and thinking, *Why do I mind*

172

that Simon Driscott is hanging out with
another girl? If we are just sort of friends
with no fancying going on whatsoever, then
why do I care?

Then I had a

TOTAL REVELATION

which was that it's because I like SD as *more* than
just a sort of friend with no fancying going on
whatsoever! In fact, I like him as a proper *boy*-type
boy *with* fancying going on (whatsoever)! I had no
idea what to do about this Utter Revelation – like,
I didn't know whether to tell Jules and Tilda, or
whether to try and squash the thought back into
nothingness, because of course I knew SD didn't
like ME apart from as a friend so there was no point
even thinking it. My mind was in a tumultuous
turmoil of confusedness, but just then Mrs. Stepton

got on the mike and I had to concentrate on her instead of on my whirly thoughts. She had a lovely spangly evening dress on and matching sparkly shoes and she hardly looked teachery at all. In fact, if you didn't already know she was a teacher you would have thought she was just a normal person! She welcomed everyone and announced that Isabella and Gabriel would do a demo to inspire everyone before the dancing competition.

Well, I can't really describe here how amazing they were. The best thing is probably if you just close your eyes and imagine Isabella in her red dress with red flowers in her black hair and loads of amazing dark eye make-up, being twirled and whirled around by Gabriel, who was wearing all black, and both of them were looking really Spanishly fiery and passionate. Then you will get what I mean.

Okay. If you are reading this bit I will assume you have opened your eyes again (duh, obviously!) so I will carry on.

After the demonstration we had a go at the waltz, jive, tango and salsa, and Isabella and Gabriel walked round the edge of the dance floor with Mrs. Stepton, to pick the winners of the competition. Some of the boys got really competitive and kept steering the girls to dance right in front of them. Jules and Cosmo were arguing about the steps as they went round, so I didn't think they would win, but Tilda and Sanjit were gliding round gracefully in the waltz and I thought they had a good chance. It was quite fun dancing with Ryan once I learned how to keep my toes out of the way of his giant clumping feet, and jiving to the rock and roll songs was brilliant because I could go spinning and twirling on my own a lot and I didn't have to stay glued to him.

Simon Driscott and Carrie won in the end (typical!), and they got 2 Splash World tickets and a Cool Cats voucher each. I did clapping with

everyone else but when Simon put his arm
round Carrie and they took a bow together my
stomach flipped over and over as if I had eaten
a dodgy prawn 'cos of it being *her* with him and
not me.

We had the food then and it was really delish
and also cool 'cos now the dancing was over
people weren't hanging out with their dates as
much. Me, Jules, Cosmo, Tilda and Sanjit got in
the queue together and Ryan went off with his
footie mates. When we reached the box for the
prom queen and king, I voted for Tilda and Sanjit
'cos Tilda just looked so amazing and plus she is
such a lovely, kind, sweet person and also Sanj
is v. v. brave 'cos he survived Mr. Van der Zwan's
scariness.

Then the DJ got the
disco music going, and
the spotlights went out
and we just had
flashing disco lights.

Us BFF and Sanj were all dancing in a big group, with Liana Hawley's lot and the okayish boys from our class, and then Simon Driscott joined in the group and then DJ Dekz put on a slow dance. I was about to go and get a drink (I wanted to try all three types and I did in the end. The Tropical Paradise was my fave!) but then Simon asked ME to dance. I looked around but I couldn't see the dance-partner thief anywhere. "What about Carrie?" I asked.

Simon shrugged his shoulders, looking really embarrassed, and mumbled, "She dumped me as soon as we'd won the dance competition. Apparently she fancies this lifeguard at Splash World, so that's why she was desperate to win the tickets. In fact she borrowed a phrase from you and called me a Prince of Pillockdom…thanks for saying that in front of the whole year group, by the way."

I felt really bad remembering that I had said that, and I really wanted to deck Carrie until she fell down a manhole for being so horrible to him. "I didn't mean it like that," I explained. "And technically I said you *used* to be one. I was actually trying to help, by rescuing you from those other girls. It's just sometimes stupid stuff comes out of my mouth before my brain has time to stop it."

"I know," said Simon, raising an eyebrow. "That's why I went off with Carrie, because I was really annoyed with you for saying it. But, oh well, I suppose your runaway mouth is just part of your essential Lucy-ness and if we're going to be sort of friends with no fancying going on whatsoever, as you so charmingly put it, I should probably get used to it."

Of course, I didn't want to be just sort of friends any more, but I didn't know how to even begin to explain that to Simon, and I didn't want to get embarrassingly rejected in front of everyone either. I just stood there, getting lost in all those thoughts racing through my mind until he waved his hands in front of my face and said, "Earth to

Planet Lucy! So, how about that dance, then?"

So we started dancing and as we were going round and round I was thinking back to the school disco one year ago when Simon tried to kiss me. I had forgotten all about it 'cos he insisted later that he had just accidentally slipped on some spilled Coke and that his lips had just unfortunately landed on my face. But then I was wondering if that was just an excuse and if he *did* in fact fancy me after all.

I realized that, like in Mrs. Stepton's science lessons, I could do an *experiment* to test my *theory* about Simon liking me to see if there was any *evidence* for it. So I called up all my courage, and then I leaned towards him and he was going, "Lucy, what are you doing?" and I was like, "Duh! Science, obviously!" and then I kissed him. And guess what? He didn't run away or be sick or anything, but in fact he kissed me back!

And then we were going, "But you don't like me!" "No, *you* don't like *me*!" and Simon explained how he had tried to ask me to the prom loads of times, but when I didn't say yes he thought I didn't want to go with him (of course, being intensely immensely *dense*, I hadn't even realized he was asking!). And I said how I was about to ask him in the dance lesson but he got in a mood with me and asked Carrie instead. And he said, "But I only did that 'cos you had just announced to everyone what you thought of me," and I said that I hadn't realized then that I did fancy him and also sorry again for the Prince of Pillockdom comment and how I don't think that any more anyway. Then Simon admitted that — aha! — he had been having secret ballroom dancing lessons every night to try and impress *me*!

So we hung round together most of the time after that, with Jules and Tilda, and Carrie ended up back together with Ryan (phew!). Jules was completely in FLABBERGASTED

GOBSMACKEDNESS about
me and Simon standing there
with our arms round each
other, but Tilda just did
this non-surprised smile
and said she had thought we
liked each other for ages.
Typical of her to realize
before *I* even did! They
did tease me a bit, saying
I would have to start
liking *Dungeons and
Dragons* and *Star Trek*
and computers to be
Simon's girlfriend, and
I went really massively bright red as a beetroot
when they said the G word. I don't know if we
are going out or not, but I would maybe like to,
so long as SD keeps his hair in the new style and
the Geeky Minions don't put an intergalactic jinx
on me for taking up some of their leader's time.

I guess we'll have to see on Monday!

Well, that's about all that hap—

Oh, I nearly forgot! Tilda was voted the prom queen (with Jamie Cousins for king, the big-head). I opened the envelope from Gladys and Beryl onstage and I was going to announce the results straight away but then I was just staring at the bit of paper for a second and absolutely grinning so much I couldn't speak. When I announced it, everyone clapped and cheered (well apart from Carrie, of course!), and the boys were trying to do extra-loud wolf whistles by sticking their fingers in their mouths. Tilda looked utterly shocked, liked she absolutely couldn't believe it, and Jules had to give her a shove to get her onto the stage. She told us later that she didn't think most of the kids in our year even knew who she was, let alone wanted to vote for her, and she was in a daze of amazement. I put the tiara on her head and she was so happy and she looked even more beautiful than ever, and me and Jules clapped the hardest of everyone. Tilda slept wearing the tiara and she went home wearing it this morning (she didn't even take it off to go in the shower!).

And something really secret for girls' ears only happened this morning as well. When I woke up I had a bit of a tummy ache, and I thought it was just too many canapés and fruit cocktails, but when I went to the bathroom I found out that it was in fact my Q arriving at last! That's *soooooo* cool! And plus 'cos my **BFF** were here I could tell them straight away (after I had told Mum and she had given me some stuff for it, of course!).

So I guess that is all of the news. Oh, except that this morning me, Jules and Tilda were sitting round the table making up different breakfast cereal mixes, and talking about the prom and whether we might be actually going out with our dates now or not (Tilda is officially **NOT** of course, especially if Mr. V is asking!) when I realized that if it is one year since the school disco, when I gave Tilda a makeover, then it must also be one year since we all three became **BFF**. Then we were all talking about the amazing stuff we have done together in this single year, like going up to London when I won the Fantasy Fashion comp and being on TV talking about our planet-friendly makeover of Tilda's bedroom, and putting on a catwalk show and creating a secret Style School and throwing a birthday party for Tilda and a Rock Party for Dad, and styling a boy band and performing in the Battle of the Bands competition and going on holiday together and dancing onstage with Jess Moon and even being in a movie! I said, "Hey girls, I hope the next year of our **BFF**ness will be as much fun as this year has been!"

We decided to celebrate being **BFF** for one whole year, so I asked Mum and she let us put a birthday candle from the drawer on one of her Belgian chocolate brownies and I lit it with the kitchen matches. Then we all held hands and decided on a joint wish. As we blew out the candle we all closed our eyes and wished to be…

Love from *your* friend,

The Totally Lucy Quiz!

So how much do you know about Lucy and her BFF? Are you a fab fan or completely clueless?
Answer the questions to find out!

1. What does Lucy call Simon Driscott's friends?

2. What is Tilda's full name?

3. In which book do Lucy, Jules and Tilda enter a dance competition?

4. In *Fantasy Fashion*, Lucy has a *hsurc terces* on someone she calls Dog Boy. But what's his real name?

5. What is Jules's signature style?

6. How many girls join Lucy's Style School in the loos? (And you get an extra point for naming them all!)

7. Who gave Lucy her own sewing machine as a birthday present?

8. In *Planet Fashion*, what colours do the girls paint Tilda's room? (Get an extra point for naming the exact paint colours!)

9. What made-up phrase does Lucy use to mean that she's over the moon?

10. Match the object with the person:

Tilda

Lucy

Jules

Mr. Cain

Alex

Simon Driscott

 BONUS ULTRA-FAN QUESTION:
When does Lucy first realize that Simon Driscott is a quite funny boy and okay, and not the Prince of Pillockdom?

Now check your answers...

1. The Geeky Minions
2. Matilda-Jane Van der Zwan
3. *Summer Stars*
4. Austin
5. Goth Rock Chick
6. 4 — Jemma, Lizzie, Carla and Sunny
7. Nan (aka Delia)
8. Purple and yellow (Purple Haze and Zanzibar)
9. *Skipping Through The Tulips*

10. Tilda — maths extension workbook
Lucy — Strawberry Burst lipgloss
Mr. Cain — single hairy eyebrow
Jules — cheese sandwich
Alex — Harry Potter hat
Simon Driscott — computer mouse

BONUS ULTRA-FAN QUESTION:
When Simon refers to Jules and
Tilda as Vampire Girl and the
Windmill Kid (p98 in *Fantasy
Fashion*, to be precise!)

☆   ☆   ☆

So, how many points did you get?
If you got the full 18 out of 18 (including the
answer to the BONUS ULTRA-FAN QUESTION),
then you could even be

☆ <u>THE</u> ACTUAL NUMBER ONE ☆
TOTALLY LUCY FAN!

Which means you almost know more about
Lucy's world than she does! Treat yourself
to a Belgian chocolate brownie!

Also, why not try out the Totally Lucy quiz
on your friends and see how they score?

☆ Totally Secret Info about ☆ Kelly McKain

Lives: In a small flat in Chiswick, West London, with a fridge full of chocolate.

Life's ambition: To be a showgirl in Paris 100 years ago. *(Erm, not really possible that one! – Ed.)* Okay, then, to be a writer – so I am actually doing it – yay! And also, to go on a flying trapeze.

Star sign: Capricorn (we're meant to be practical).

Fave colour: Purple.

Fave animal: Monkey.

Ideal pet: A purple monkey.

My Best Friends Forever: The totally fantabulous Helen and Laura – we all grew up on the same street and have shared all kinds of CRINGES together, including once thinking it was a good idea to wear matching bright pink jumpsuits!

Fave hobbies: Hanging out with my BFF and gorge boyf, watching *Friends*, going to yoga and dance classes, and playing my guitar as badly as Lucy's dad!

Have you read all of Lucy's hilarious journals?

Makeover Magic
Lucy tries her makeover magic on the shy new girl at school.
9780746066898

Fantasy Fashion
Can Lucy design a fab enough outfit to win a fashion comp?
9780746066904

Boy Band Blues
Lucy's thrilled to be asked to style a boy band for a school comp.
9780746066911

Star Struck
Lucy's in an actual film! Can she get her cool designs noticed?
9780746070611

Picture Perfect
Will crossed wires ruin Lucy's plans for a surprise birthday party?
9780746070628

Style School
Lucy's started a secret Style School club, but will Mr. Cain find out?
9780746070635

Summer Stars
The girls enter a beach party dance comp together on their hols!
9780746080177

Catwalk Crazy
Can Lucy uncover the secret saboteur of her charity fashion show?
9780746080184

Planet Fashion
Will Lucy's planet-friendly makeover on Tilda's bedroom get on TV?
9780746080191

If you love Kelly McKain, look out for her exciting new book, coming next year...

Keep an eye on Kelly's website for more info!

☆ www.kellymckain.co.uk ☆

This book is for all the totally fab Lucy fans
across the world – you are just such
a brilliant bunch of girls!
Mwah! xx

First published in the UK in 2008 by Usborne Publishing Ltd., Usborne House,
83-85 Saffron Hill, London EC1N 8RT, England. www.usborne.com

Text copyright © Kelly McKain, 2008.
Illustrations copyright © Usborne Publishing Ltd., 2008

The right of Kelly McKain to be identified as the author of this work has been
asserted by her in accordance with the Copyright, Designs and Patents Act, 1988.

Illustrations by Vici Leyhane.
Photography: (Page 9) Couple at prom © Image Source/Getty Images;
trio of girls © Polka Dot Images/SuperStock. (Page 21) Woman with chandelier
© DreamPictures/Image Bank/Getty Images; woman in striped dress © Plush
Studios/Photodisc/Getty Images. (Page 22) Woman stepping out of limo ©
George Doyle/Stockbyte/Getty Images.

The name Usborne and the devices 🔔 🐝 are Trade Marks of Usborne Publishing
Ltd.

This is a work of fiction. The characters, incidents, and dialogues are
products of the author's imagination and are not to be construed as real.
Any resemblance to actual events or persons, living or dead, is entirely
coincidental.

A CIP catalogue record for this book is available from the British Library.

JFMAMJ ASOND/17 01866/08   ISBN 9780746080207   Printed in India